PADDLE SHOTS
A River Pretty Anthology, Vol. 2
Spring 2016

Edited by Lee Busby & Richard Farrell

Front and back cover illustrations by Chaz Miller

© 2016 Busby & Farrell. All Rights Reserved.

ISBN 978-1-329-95593-6

Contents

Acknowledgments

Forward by RICHARD FARRELL & LEE BUSBY

Introduction by RICHARD JACKSON

Excerpt from *TRAVERSINGS* by RICHARD JACKSON & ROBERT VIVIAN 1

JOHN ABERNATHY	*You're an Abernathy* 4
C D ALBIN	*Traveling Mercies* 11
KELLI ALLEN	*Between Your Hand and Some Answer* 24
LAURA BAIRD	*Moving* 25
IAN BODKIN	*Consume* 26
NIKKI BOSS	*Impossible* 29
MICHAEL BRASIER	*Falling Through the Cracks* 31
KAREN BURTON	*In Fourteen Seconds* 33
NATALIE BYERS	*King of Center Creek* 36
	Richard Jackson Writes About Love and Traps Robert Vivian in a Poem 38
MARCUS CAFAGÑA	*The Law of Gravity* 40

KATCH CAMPBELL	*Written in the Book of Life* 42
BARBARA SIEGEL CARLSON	*The Pear* 43
KITTY CARPENTER	*Between Silences* 45
DEREK COWSERT	*Fire Places* 46
CHRIS CRABTREE	*Traveling to Tecumseh, Missouri* 59
JODRAN CULOTTA	*For Kelly* 60
KRISTEN CYPRET	*Coping* 62
JIM DANIELS	*Last Day in Coldwater* 64
	If You Ever Have To Do This Yourself 66
CARRIE DIMINO	*Missouri to Kansas: The Work Road* 67
GREGORY DONOVAN	*Besides* 68
	The Grandfather in the Rafters 69
ALTA LEAH EMRICK	*River Pretty Makeover* 71
BRANDON FUNK	*Iambic Cento* 73
D. GILSON	*A History of My Father as the History of McDonald's* 74

HUNTER HOBBS	*Where I Left My Coat* 76
JIMMY HUFF	*Who Cooks for You? Who Cooks for Y'all?* 77
ROBERT HYERS	*Bosom Buddies* 85
ELIZABETH HYKES	*Hand Blown in Ohio* 91
KELLY JOLENE	*An Infection* 93
MATTHEW KIMBERLIN	*Masks* 94
MARY KNOBBE	*Michaella* 103
TIMOTHY LEYRSON	*The Genesis* 105
ANDREW MARSHALL	*Black Crickets* 107
JOHN MONAGLE	*Sitting on the Ledge* 108
ANNIE NEWCOMER	*An Emotional Response to C.K. Williams' "Near the Haunted Castle" In a Workshop at River Pretty* 109
BILL OAKLEY	*Losing Things I Love Through Inattention* 111 *Little Tiny Hand Jobs* 112
TODD OSBORNE	*Counting Rings* 113

J.T. ROBERTSON	*While Skimming Requests for Proposals* 114
ALLEN ROSS	*Sun Chips* 117
	A Lifetime of Memories with the Sticky Food Group 118
SOPHFRONIA SCOTT	*The Payoff Letter* 120
HEATHER SHARFEDDIN	*Gift Giving in America: A Guide* 124
SUE WILLIAM SILVERMAN	*If Love Is Here Every Day!* 140
SIERRA SITZES	*The Baptism of Anna Spence* 142
ANDY SMART	*Uphill with Lady* 151
DEBBIE THEISS	*Second Chance?* 152
MICHAELLA A THORNTON	*After the Final No* 153
ROBERT VIVIAN	*Clouds Above the River* 156
JAN WAY	*Short Shots* 157

Acknowledgments

WE WOULD LIKE to thank the asteroids, the blue skies and roaring river, the trees, the possums, the makers of wine and whiskey, the bats in the rafters, the writers toiling away day after day, the mill for holding up, the cooks, the bartender for being so polite, the Doc, and especially you and you and you for being a part of this journey.

Forward

HERE, RICH SAYS something great and makes both himself and Lee look and feel good. Or here, Lee acknowledges that after five years, River Pretty has grown beyond our wildest dreams. Lee does indeed acknowledge such a mind-blowing milestone, and casually reflects, with pride, at how the community has grown and spread across the United States. Rich pontificates about the writing life: The writing life. Well, it seems to me that the writing comes to life at River Pretty, over three magical days of inspiration, fellowship, and mindful work. And then Lee Busby talks about the Gravel Bar's little known fact: you get a free drink for every cartwheel that you land correctly - you must be 21 to enter and land on your feet without a wobble. There's rumor that a poet pulled off this magical feat at RP3, but all records and proof has since been lost. Here, Rich pontificates again and again: Isn't that what we are all doing? Trying to pull off the perfect cartwheel? Trying to land on our feet without a wobble? *Paddle Shots Vol. 2* captures more than forty perfect cartwheels with flawless landings in the shape of poems, essays, and stories. The only question that remains: Is Lee buying the beers? And some questions are better left unanswered. So sit back, pull up a foot stool, take a long drink of your favorite watered-down beverage and enjoy the hell out of these fantastic works of art.

--Rich and Lee

FILLING THE CUP

"I'VE FOUND IT TAKES LOVE to fill an empty cup," writes Jordan Culotta in a poem included in this edition of *Paddleshots*, and the proof is here in these poems, and in fact overflows with an enormous variety of expressions. When I read a poem, any piece of creative writing, when I look at art or listen to music, I am interested not so much in the themes but the *way* the artists think and feel. The themes I can get in philosophy, history or religion texts, but the way someone thinks and feels, if I can somehow enter that process then I have expanded my own self, have seen the world through different eyes have found yet another way to fill that empty cup.

Kelli Allen also gives us something like this in her poem where she says:

> We arrived identically with our backs pressed,
> a confluence, and there was nothing in that bourbon bottle
> that could lessen what I heard you say, your wooden horse
> all at once the color of some midnight sun.

This is an anthology where we all arrive at some place like that, maybe one of the places listed in Jordan's poem, maybe it is a process, as Laura Baird says, of "this moving towards you until the conversation we make as evening falls," resulting in what she calls a "mystery" which is always the immeasurable depths of our hearts. It becomes apparent in the way Karen Burton seems to inhale the world around her as if it were pure spirit.

So it is the voice, then, the way, the spirit that is conveyed through language—listen to Barbara Carlson:

I love to say *angel hair*, imagining the soft
light body of a god slipping down my throat.
A divine hum on my tongue, a slight thing, a
sensation.

But it is not just the voice but the unsayable that lies behind words, shadows them for, as Kitty Carpenter says, "Between silences / long fingers of shadow brush my shoulders," and Jim Daniels mentions "Listening to the blue music / of our veins." Hunter Hobbs suggests that this unsayable arises out of our intense desire to somehow fill that empty cup of loss: "surely there's a word / for us--something like / desperate--but quieter."

Reading through these poems to be introduced to new visions, to begin to understand the innumerable depths, paths of seeing, fields of feeling that make up what it means to be human. We are on this road, as Chris Crabtree says, that "curves with the contour of the land," taking us to unexpected places where we discover ourselves and the world anew. In this time of political lies, skepticism, and isolationism it is what will save us if we can be saved.

-RICHARD JACKSON

PADDLE SHOTS
A River Pretty Anthology, Vol. 2
Spring 2016

The following excerpt is from the book *TRAVERSINGS* (Anchor & Plume 2016) by RICHARD JACKSON AND ROBERT VIVAN – a collection that was first conceptualized at the River Pretty Writers Retreat

Not Here (RJ)

The moon only rehearses what the day has taught it. The last rooks map again the wind's currents. Time is measured here by the loudening voices of tree frogs. Earlier, the bear and I stood across the ravine exchanging shadows the way lovers do in those medieval romances.
Neither of us cared that a planet thirty three light years away shed its atmosphere in a trail of gasses 9 million miles long, nor worried when that would happen here. What we were waiting for was the annual June show of fireflies who synchronize themselves into trailing ribbons of light undulating back and forth through the woods. It is a way of saying we are here, we are one, a romance of light. Through the lattice work of branches we watched another universe take shape. Beyond, the skeletons of a failed village was becoming its own forest. Now and then a coyote claimed its own space. A few shy stars seemed humbled by it all. A few bats seemed confused by echoes from what they must have thought was a flying snake. Hypnotized maybe.
Was it a coincidence we met there, two beings from different worlds amazed at how those undulations guided the beating of our one heart? He turned away then as reverently as from an altar. For a moment the earth tottered on its axis. I don't think you can love the world any more than this, each of our breaths trailing off into a night that will never know we were here.

Waving To The Dead (RV)

From a lifetime ago and how they do not wave back, wave forward but wait ever deeper in the ground leaning and tilting toward earth's axis and turning the tiny chock wheels that make the grass grow, oh, the mighty turning and waving to the dead fey gesture of utter futility though there's some hope and music in it, the threadbare sighing that floats above them above us all and physical reaching out and what would you do with your hands all the lifelong days, what would you do remembering and dreaming of the dead, conjuring them almost in verse and story and high up moaning, my dead and your dead and all the perished and cherished lost ones who are blazing a dark and silent trail we must follow, must follow and not who will wave to me when I am gone but whose hands will hold a teacup or close the iron gates or caress the naked body of a trembling lover, oh, the love and life of this and may your waving live forever but for now the touch of a fly rod or the chin of my niece who lights the way for all of us in what must be the smile of holy traverse as I wave to the dead again with the water of my hand, the one so uncertain of connecting or getting through and the one that knows to touch and to hold is a prayer made manifest of flesh, oh, bag of cherries or the door to a library where the books wait in dusty silence like vivid graves packed with light and color waiting to burst forth and live again in any aching human breast.

Contrapuntal (RJ & RV)

Only last week's newspaper and his sack lunch cradled by the park bench.

And how he waits, cambered and hunched over, belabored, fallen, fallen.

Like Newton's apple, crossing the sunlight, suspended in mid air.

And this core of the world, or any world, held in rapt abeyance.

But the soul, the soul is a kite broken loose from its string.

No destination wheat in those pages, no light, only other, and distant bloom.

Except the ragman collecting fallen petals of moonlight.

All exeunt begins as the rags begin to glow, the black ink blurring like wine.

Beneath the bench a moth has set a funnel of a grass spider's web trembling.

Who is he when the spider dust settles, web lacing itself to hold and to kill/love?

The souls that fly off, we call them moths by the bad grammar of our lives.

So flutter, flutter now, the wayfarer seekers and double negatives turning into song.

The owl that wants to be the moon knows Paradise is a life you've hidden from yourself.

Before the light freezes me I tell the river I won't let a window kill me.

John Abernathy

You're an Abernathy

SON. MAX. COME INSIDE for a second, ok? Because I say so. You can go right back out when we're done but... just come inside. Max. Now! You ok? You need more sunscreen? Your cheeks are a little red. No let's get you some more sunscreen first. This is... this is actually what I wanted to talk to you about.

We've got a vacation coming up, right? In a couple weeks? Well, your mom and I have decided to take a trip. All of us. We're going on vacation.

Not... no not Disney again. Not camping. No, no more museums but really I don't appreciate that tone, we had a good time. Remember the science place? Remember the art? Well, sure, the place with all the naked lady paintings but that's not... never mind. That's not important. We're going somewhere different this vacation, somewhere new. It's a place you've...

Yeah. Yeah it's the beach.

Ok. Hey alright. It's exciting. I know just...

Hey calm down for a...

Ok...

Max...

I know, very exciting, but you need to know something. Are you listening? Are you paying attention? This isn't going to be like other vacations. There's something you need to know about your old man, ok? Something to need to know about yourself.

You're an Abernathy, son. I can only protect you from that for so long. Someday, someday soon in fact, the minute we step onto that beach, that's going to mean something to you.

Something bad. No, wait, it doesn't have to be scary. Sorry. Sorry. Look at you. Damn—sorry, darn. Sorry.

Hey let's take a step back, ok? You know who the Scottish are? The Nords? The Vikings? Yeah, not yet, but that's where we come from, where all the old Abernathys used to live. They're all cloudy, cold, sunless places. Places that don't have beaches, not beaches like we have, anyway. Well, there's this thing that happens called genetics where you get the things your parents had, and they get what your grandparents had, and they get what your great grandparents had, and so on and so on… and you know what they all had?

Lots of cloud cover.

The beach isn't what you think it is. You have this commercialized vision of it, all ads and… oh, I guess it means kind of fake? Pretend? Not completely real. It means the beach has been made up all pretty to sell you something, to sell you the beach, but it's not true. Or maybe there are other truths, other things they don't tell you.

Well, lots of things. Tell me what you think you know about the beach and I'll tell you how it's wrong.

Yeah, there's lots of that but...

No it doesn't exactly work that way. You can't build them that big. That's just in cartoons. No really, you can't even walk around inside them. Because sand is like Legos but worse. Imagine a pile of tiny Legos that don't really click together but do stick to each other just well enough to get your hopes up. It *seems* like clay, it *seems* like it's going to do what you want, but it's lying to you. Yeah. Sand is a liar son. The moment you start to trust it, the moment you're getting along well enough, it'll collapse. All your walls, all your turrets, all your time completely wasted. All that hard work will crumble into the mote, melt into the water, and you'll have nothing to do but stomp it flat and start all over again. Then…

Yeah you can make a moat. Moats are pretty easy actually. And, yeah, the stomping's pretty fun. No, not a complete waste of time I guess, but you're missing the point.

You're not really thinking about what the sand's going to be like. Remember the sandbox at the Jungle Center? You never played in it, right? Why not?

No, that's not true at all. You hated that sandbox. Max, come on, I watch you play! I once saw you drag a chair all the way across a playground so you could sit on the edge of the sandbox and dig instead of getting inside it. Now seriously, why didn't you want to sit in the sandbox?

Yeah, very sticky. Yeah, *very* gross. Oh yeah, and not just in your shoes. In your socks, in your pants, in your hair, sand was everywhere right? Well what do you think the beach is going to be like? How is an entire coast of sand going to be better than a little box? You'll sweat. You'll come out of the ocean dripping wet. It'll stick to you like it's trying to turn you sandpaper. It'll be in your ears, on your face, up your nose. You'll be picking gritty sand boogers for a week.

But it's not the sand alone that's gross, is it?

Remember what else happened in the sandbox? Remember what you found? Yeah. Poops. All the time, poops. Yeah, from cats. Well at the beach there's something worse than cats—people. Just imagine, son, maybe you decide to dig a shallow little grave and bury yourself up to the neck and—oh yeah, on the beach that's a normal thing, you know? People do that for fun, bury themselves alive and cover themselves in sticky grit—but while you're digging this hole, with each successive shovelful of sand you're also pulling up plastic bags, half eaten food trash, used diapers, cigar butts, shards of glass, soda can tabs, bottle tops, needles…

Yeah, of course there are trash cans, people just choose not to use them. I'm not sure why, son, they're probably just assholes—sorry, buttheads. Actually don't say buttheads either.

Anyway, there's something even worse than the sand at the beach, and almost as bad as the people... the Sun. Your mother... well she doesn't have to worry about it so much. Her side of the family all brown up like toast as soon as the Sun hits them, they just sit there all day... tanning. Yeah. You just sit in the sun and get hot and turn brown. Brown. Hell—sorry, heck—I don't know why. I can't spend more than fifteen minutes in the sun before I start to turn red and... no, no red is not cooler than brown. Red is a burn. Yeah like on the stove.

I guess it's just because we have different kinds of skin. Your mom's skin can stand the sun and mine just blisters underneath it. You want to...? Oh. The thing is son, you don't really get to pick which skin you have. It just happens. Remember genetics? You're born with it. Well, let's not call it God, Abernathy's already have enough to blame on Him. Call it body science. Like, you have eyes just like your mom's, and skin just like mine!

No, you can't switch.

Look, we're getting distracted. Remember tee-ball? You spent most of the time in the dugout. And the park? Gazebos, trees, shade. Always shade. And despite it we still had to put you in long sleeves. In July. And that cowboy hat wasn't just for fun. And what about the lake, or Splash Planet last Labor Day? Well at the beach.... *there is no shade*. Sure you can put up a little umbrella, and you'll get a four-square-foot prison of shadow that's constantly moving down the beach, uncovering you, leaving half of you to bake in the sun.

The thing is, it doesn't even matter. The sand is in cahoots with the sun. It *reflects* the sun right back up at you. It's like a mirror, so the sun comes at you from above *and* below until your only hope... is sunscreen. Lots and lots of sunscreen.

No. *No.* I do *not* put it on too thick. That's exactly how... *no.* Son you have to let it sit for... *you have to let it sit* for an hour!

Yes you do! It says so on the... ok, you know what, you just wait right here.

Ok, look. Read this... right here. *Before applying Kabuki Brand Sunscreen, first consider whether you really need to go outside. If unavoidable, apply 1.5 oz. (minimum) evenly across exposed areas and allow to cure for one hour before entering sunlight. Waterproof, more or less, but we wouldn't suggest it. Reapply after two-to-three hours or as soon as skin returns to a natural pallor. Safe for daily use, ideal for summertime miming.*

Yes, it really says that. Here, take it. See? What? That stands for Sun Protection Factor. Do you know what this big number is? Yeah, fifty-five. And this little one? That's called an *exponent*, you'll learn about that in algebra someday.

Look I'm... *no I'm not*. Son just calm down a little. I'm not trying to ruin the beach. I'm not trying to scare you. I don't want to... here, wipe your nose. I don't want you to be scared of anything, there's just so much you should be prepared for. *You're an Abernathy*, so you'll probably sweat all that sunscreen off in just twenty or thirty minutes. We'll be reapplying a lot. You'll likely burn anyway, so you'll have to deal with aloe, maybe even some blisters and an oatmeal bath. Yeah. Exactly what it sounds like. It's going to be hot and humid and sandy and salty and it's *all* going to get in your eyes at some point... but son there's something else you're going to have to deal with. Me.

There comes a point in every young man's life when he sees his father fall off his altar. What I mean is, you still kind of see me as a superhero. As invincible. As more than human. I just don't want you to be too disappointed when, inevitably, I don't stand up to that image anymore.

You see son, there's only one way I know how to enjoy the beach. There's only one thing that makes the whole production worthwhile and it's not... it's not pretty. I walk out to where waves break and just wait. Then, as the biggest, toughest, angriest waves crest and fall before me, I toss myself into them like some kind of rag doll, like a sacrifice to Neptune.

Right. Ariel's dad.

Well I... I don't know why. The wave grabs me, twists me around, slams me against the ocean floor, and then drops me off several feet closer to the shore. Sometimes I'm hit again before I can even wipe my eyes or catch my breath. Eventually I end up back at the beach, or at least close enough that the waves can't affect me, so I walk back out and wait for another big one.

I do this for hours. Every day. Son? Just checking. You had this weird look. I get it. When I leave the beach I have as many friction burns as sun burns. Also I'm some kind of magnet for jellyfish and crabs—I hope that's not genetic, too—so I almost always come away from a beach vacations looking like I lost a fight.

I guess what I'm saying is, prepare yourself. You don't have to enjoy the beach the same way I do or your mother does but… Oh she stretches out like a monument on the shore and quietly reads until it's time for seafood. Sometimes she goes on walks. Yeah, it does seem better, doesn't it? But that's the point. You can't expect to have that experience. You're an Abernathy. You're going to find a *lot* of things at the beach to bother you. Gritty, stinging, burning, itching, wet, sticky, sweaty things... rednecks, trailer trash, college students, all with incredibly loud, awful music, all of them way too fat or way too fit, and all of them, worst of all, having fun. Somehow, impossibly, each managing to have a really great time while you curl up under a towel, despite the heat, and count the minutes until you get to go back into the air conditioning.

Or maybe you're not there yet. Maybe I'm just projecting.

Well, it means I'm seeing a little bit of myself in you, which is why I had you come in here in the first place I guess. Try not to think about it too much. Let's put some more sunscreen on—yes, *even* more—before you go back outside.

Tonight we'll go buy you a beach towel, and maybe a hoodie. Trust me.

C.D. Albin

Traveling Mercies

RAY DENTON FIRST noticed the catch in his fuel line an hour northwest of Memphis, but he continued on, hoping he could make it across the river into the city before the worrisome slip in the car's power became too serious. Not once in his life had he broken down along a highway, and he told himself, mantra-like, that his luck would hold. Twenty minutes later the engine began firing so intermittently he barely made it to the exit ramp outside Ajax, Arkansas, a town he thought he might have stopped in once for fuel. Leaning close to the steering wheel, he coaxed the Impala off the ramp into a thin stream of Thursday afternoon traffic, but the engine cut out again, the whole vehicle shuddering maddeningly before slowing to a crawl. Soon cars began to swerve around him, forcing him to pull onto the narrow shoulder. When he opened his door a crack, a horn blared through like a punch in his ear.

Flinching, Ray looked at the cell phone on the seat beside him. He'd never joined AAA and knew no one to call in Ajax. For a moment he considered dialing his office at Ozark Mountain Community College, where he was Dean, but there was nothing Fern, his assistant, could do from a hundred miles away. Ahead he spotted a Wendy's sign, and beyond that what looked like a service station. Slipping the phone in his pocket, he glanced at his new suit stretched across the back seat and then down at his freshly shined loafers before stepping cautiously onto the blacktop. A hot wind blew past, and he hurried to the front of the Impala while a pickup pounded by, buffeting him in its wake. By the time he reached the Wendy's parking lot his shirt was damp, sweat pooling over his eyebrows, but Ajax Automotive lay just ahead.

Heavy odors of grease and gasoline spoiled the air as Ray approached the three-bay garage, where somewhere in back a steely tool pinged off concrete. In the first bay a mechanic rattled the loose muffler of a blue sedan before stepping directly beneath the undercarriage for a better look. Ray shuddered, imagining the rack buckling, the car coming down on the mechanic's body.

"Help you?" barked a heavy-set man. Grateful for the offer, Ray followed the man's wave as he motioned toward an open door. Once inside Ray found no place to sit, only a counter and cash register, the back wall lined with shelves of chips and candy bars. The man settled himself behind the counter and scratched a salt-and-pepper goatee. A name patch with a red *Stan* embroidered in cursive perched like a miniature billboard above his chest pocket.

"My car died back there," Ray said. "I think it could be the fuel line."

Stan rolled a wrist, checking his watch. "We can tow it. Maybe get you going in the morning."

Ray groaned. "I need to get to my hotel. I have a job interview tomorrow, in Memphis."

Stan said nothing, and Ray recognized the glazed inattention he often associated with Wal-Mart cashiers and supermarket clerks, employees he assumed endured each shift wishing only to get home to families and television sets. He turned and studied the Wendy's across the way, where people in dependable vehicles idled in the drive-through lane. "What's the chance of a ride?"

Stan shrugged. "Trace might do it after we close. I'll check when he pulls your car."

Ray handed over his keys. Outside he blinked into the sun and waited by the gas pumps. Soon the Impala glided in behind a shiny red and white wrecker, *Ajax Automotive* painted prominently on the doors. Stan met the driver and jabbed a thumb in Ray's direction, gesturing toward the highway as he talked. When Stan finished and retreated to the garage, the driver gave Ray half a wave. Ray approached, guessing the man to be thirty or so, noting the blond stubble that shadowed his face. A grimy Memphis Redbirds cap counterpointed a blue work shirt and matching trousers, both streaked with grime.

"Trace Shipley," the man said. "Sounds like you're having some trouble."

"I'm afraid so. My car died."

"Yeah. Pinches when your rig breaks down."

Ray pointed back toward the garage. "Your boss? He said you might take me on to Memphis. I can pay."

Trace sighed and stared at an oily patch of concrete as if something in the stain worried him. When he looked up, his forehead was furrowed. "Think you could spare a hundred?" he asked. "I'm not trying to screw you. It's just if we get caught in traffic, I'll miss my boy's Little League game. He's pitching."

Ray met the man's wide, blue eyes and briefly wondered how to tell a Samaritan from a serial killer. "A hundred's fine," he said.

*

Trace's personal vehicle resembled a farm truck that had seen better days, its cream paint peeling along the hood and passenger door, an impressive dent rusting above the right rear wheel well. Ray settled his overnight bag in the middle of the seat, but there was no place to hang his suit so he folded it gently and held it on his knees like a pie bound for the county fair.

"We'll hit rush hour in West Memphis," Trace said, starting the engine to a radio blast of country music, which he punched off with the flat of his hand. "But once we're over the river there'll be more people heading out than going in."

Ray nodded, relieved to be traveling once again in the direction of his hotel room where he could hang up his suit, stretch on the bed, and collect his thoughts for tomorrow's interview at Western Tennessee. He'd need to call Teresa too. His wife wasn't thrilled about the possibility of moving to a big city like Memphis, but she hadn't made herself sick with worry either. Ray knew she doubted he'd be hired as Dean of Developmental Studies, since she thought the position too big a jump for him. *They've never heard of Ozark Mountain*, she'd said when he first told her he planned to apply. *Or you*. Then last week, when he announced he'd made the interview round, she pursed her lips as a first defense against bad news and asked how many applicants had received the same invitation. After he finally admitted he didn't know, her face relaxed into a hint of a smile. Ray concluded she was imagining a large room crowded with mid-level administrator types, all crammed shoulder-to-shoulder.

The pickup merged into traffic off the exit ramp, and a moment later a kick of acceleration settled Ray deeply into his seat. Trace flipped the turn signal and powered past a matronly lady and two young children in a Ford Escape. "We'll get you where you're going," he said, his voice solemn as a minister's.

Ray considered the speedometer, its needle rising rapidly. "No need to hurry. They'll hold my room."

Trace nodded and lifted the Redbirds cap by the bill, rubbing his forehead with the heel of his palm. A thinning hairline made him look older, more careworn than Ray first thought. "Just like to do a job right," he said.

Ray watched the speedometer settle at seventy. "That's a good quality."

Trace glanced his way. "Stan said you're looking for work. Might have a line in Memphis."

"An interview," Ray corrected. "I'm thinking it may be time for a change."

Trace smiled into the windshield. "Time for a change," he repeated, lilting the words as if they came from a favorite song. "We all get to that place, don't we?"

Ray looked down the long, flat highway, the last of Ajax's commercial properties giving way on either side to the green of cultivated fields. Back home in Lotten those fields would be pastures, horses and beef cattle dotting stony hills and steep ridges, the thin soil too stingy to nurture crops that grew in orderly, prospering rows. He thought a moment of his older brother Dale, who for years had worked full-time factory jobs, jumping at any overtime he could get just to hold onto eighty acres—hard land that had already cost him a wife, a John Deere tractor, and a back that bent without pain. Ray shook his head, wondering if the choice to stay home and build a career at Ozark Mountain had cost him just as much. "No change, no life," he said, and immediately sensed Trace give him a quick, assessing stare.

Thirty minutes later they crested a hill on the far side of West Memphis and spotted the bridge silvering in the sun. "Here we go," Trace said. "Big ol' Muddy."

Ray straightened as if he were being measured for height. Craning his neck, he waited for a glimpse of the river while Trace swept past an overburdened gravel truck to improve their entry onto the two-lane bridge. Ray had crossed the Mississippi at least a dozen times before, but now he felt a fluttering in his stomach and thought, briefly, of a bird lifting from the ground.

As always, Ray was surprised at how quickly the river could be crossed. He counted several barges in the distance and listened to the pounding of the pickup's tires, noting with satisfaction the small boundary marker in the middle of the bridge that told him Arkansas was behind him. Then they were on the other side, surging into the hurly-burly of Memphis itself.

"So where's your hotel?" Trace called over the traffic. "You'll need to point me."

Ray fumbled in his chest pocket for the directions he'd printed from his computer and noticed Trace glancing his way, eyebrows arched. "Mapquest," Ray said.

Trace swallowed, his Adam's apple rising and falling. "Okay. Fire away."

Ray spent the next few minutes glancing between the computer's directions and the city's signs, calling out exit numbers and street names until the traffic finally thinned and they needed only to navigate one stoplight and a right turn into the parking lot of the Fairmont Inn. He was swiveling his head, hoping the university might be close enough to glimpse, when Trace slammed the brakes and rocked him toward the dashboard. The seatbelt grabbed him with a jolt as a blue blur of SUV surged out of a side street, claiming the pickup's front fender in a groaning complaint of metal. Wide-eyed, Ray watched the SUV shudder across the opposite lane and nose onto the shoulder.

"Hell Fire!" Trace yelled, anger ricocheting around the cab.

Ray checked over his shoulder, fearful they might be plowed from the rear, but he saw only a handful of halted vehicles, their shocked drivers pantomiming behind sun-stippled windshields. Slumping back around, he noticed with a pang that his suit had been flung to the floorboard, his own loafers now pressing footprints into the lapels.

Trace gripped him by the shoulder, each finger a prong. "Are you hurt?"

"No. You?"

"I'm shorn a front end, that's for sure." Jumping down from the cab, Trace snatched off his cap and studied the damage until anxious drivers began to honk and crowd into the next lane, determined to pass. Exasperated, he waved them on before returning and leaning in the window. "Steer over to the shoulder, okay? I need to check on that other guy."

Ray watched him pick through traffic, then moved behind the wheel, cautiously guiding the truck to the shoulder in a slow roll that sounded like tin cans dragging from the driveshaft. He shut off the engine and stepped down amid a litter of flung glass and popped rivets, the sun instantly heating one side of his face.

Across the way, Trace helped an old man out of the SUV and steadied him against the side of the vehicle. The man kept shaking his head and talking with his hands, eventually beginning to weep. Trace gave him a couple of stiff pats on the back, then reached into his pocket and brought out a handkerchief, passing it into the old man's hands. Moments later he returned to retrieve his phone from the cab and report the accident. "I don't think he knows where he is," he told Ray. "He keeps saying they moved the stop sign on him."

Ray wondered if the man had dementia, or maybe just heat stroke. For the second time today he was sweating through his shirt, and when he turned to take in the Fairmont in the distance, the marquee shimmered with the promise of air conditioning and cable television. Immediately Ray considered handing Trace the money they had agreed on and hiking the rest of the way.

"They ought to be here soon," Trace said, ending the call. "I told them the old guy's pretty frazzled." Motioning toward the hotel, he flicked an invisible pebble over Ray's head. "There she is. You're in walking distance, at least."

Ray nearly reached for his wallet. "What about you?"

Trace let out a sigh. "Right now I got to deal with this mess. Talk to the cops, see if they can help me get a tow." He drew a forearm across his slick brow. "There goes Trey's game. He'll probably no hit 'em now, won't he?"

For the first time Ray remembered Trace's son. "How old is he?"

"Ten. Pretty good arm." Suddenly Trace caught a pulse of energy and leaned close, his voice confiding. "I'm partial though."

Nodding, Ray recalled attending a few of Michelle's middle school volleyball games. Mostly she had sat on the bench, playing only when a match became lop-sided, and even then she moved around the court tentatively, as if she preferred her teammates to control the action. Ray assumed she'd tried out merely because it was something to do, a way to be with her friends. He hadn't enjoyed the shrill shouting from some of the parents and was glad when Michelle quit after only one season, but years later she made a strange remark at the dinner table after qualifying for state competition in oral interpretation. He had asked what time her first round would be, so that he could drive down to Little Rock to hear her speech. "Don't bother, Daddy," she'd said. "You'll just be bored." When he protested, she and Teresa rolled their eyes at each other, and he felt a certain relief that he wasn't included. Yet his daughter's words had lodged like a cyst beneath the skin.

The sun poured down in a steady blast, and Ray decided he was wasting time. "I appreciate the ride," he said, pulling out his wallet. On impulse, he added an extra ten. "For your trouble."

Slowly Trace raised the bill of his cap with his thumb. "You can go broke paying for folks' troubles," he said.

Ray continued to hold out the ten. "It's the least I can do."

After a few seconds Trace took the extra bill and handed Ray the overnight bag and rumpled suit from the truck cab. Ray nodded and started for the hotel, anxious for the cool quiet of his room. The walk was longer than he anticipated and several times he shifted the bag from one hand to the other, fearful the suit would wrinkle more severely with each jostle.

Inside the lobby he waited at the reception desk until a young woman emerged from a back room and apologized while scanning her computer screen. At first she couldn't locate his reservation, and for an awful moment he wondered if Western had canceled the interview at the last minute. Then the girl's face brightened. "You're here after all," she declared, legitimizing him with duplicate key cards and directions to the elevator.

His room lay at the end of the hall on the second floor and smelled vaguely of dry-cleaning. He hung the suit in the bathroom and let the shower run hot, counting on steam to remove wrinkles. After downing a soda from the hall vending machine, he collapsed on the bed to phone home. Teresa picked up on the fifth ring.

He left out the car trouble and the wreck itself, telling her only that he'd arrived safely, that he was looking forward to the interview. "I think I have a shot," he said, although the sentiment sounded thin when he heard it from his own lips.

"Okay." Her voice was so flat he imagined her stretching an arm to inspect her fingernails. "Oh," she said. "Michelle went out tonight."

"What?"

"A movie. With Tony Edmonds."

Ray ground his teeth. He tried to recall anyone named Tony Edmonds and finally settled on a thin, mildly acned boy whose shyness offered hope Michelle would lose interest quickly. He didn't feel up to the complications his daughter's heart might engender, especially if things worked out with Western. "I meet the search committee at 11:00 tomorrow," he said.

Teresa made a sound as if she'd been sucker punched. "Then why did you go down there tonight?"

"What else would I do?"

"You could have left in the morning. You'd have plenty of time."

Ray massaged his eyelids and wished for sleep. "I have meetings scheduled from 8:00 on. I told you that."

"No you didn't."

"I'm sure I did."

Her voice lowered, took on an edge. "You're always so sure."

Pushing himself to a sitting position, he flattened his back against the headboard. "I have to stay focused, Teresa. Let's not start this again. I don't need it."

"What you don't need is that job. None of us do."

Anger surged him off the bed. "Don't start the 'us' games, okay. I've had my fill."

"What 'us'? You're the one that's off in Memphis."

"I'm trying for something better."

"For you. Nobody else wants it."

"Because you only want what you want, everything else be damned."

Her voice came higher now, wavering. "I'm not the selfish one."

"So I guess that leaves me, doesn't it?"

"You always do this."

"Do what? Keep you from running my life? It's mine. I get to choose."

Her voice was so muffled now he couldn't make out her reply, only the clear, precise click as she ended the call.

An hour later Ray sat at a bistro table in a Subway one block behind the Fairmont. He'd ordered a Spicy Italian but had finished less than half the sandwich, his nerves so jangled the food seemed an assault on his stomach. Little had gone the way he'd planned for this trip, and he knew he had to turn things around for tomorrow. Probably the best thing would be to go back to the hotel and relax, find some way to get Teresa's nonsense out of his head. At the very least, he ought to review his notes a final time.

Outside the air had cooled a bit, the evening pleasant enough he decided to cut across the grassy knoll separating the Fairmont from the strip of shops and fast food stores. He was huffing a bit by the time he made it to the top and stepped onto the parking lot, which was nearly empty. There he noticed only a young man standing near the trunk of a sports car, fishing for keys in the deep front pocket of his cargo shorts. Ray nodded in passing and heard a musical clink as the other man lifted the keys in a casual, acknowledging wave. A few steps nearer the building and Ray registered a rushing glissando in the air behind his right ear, too late to duck the blow that robbed him of his legs and sent him lurching toward the pavement.

Unable to keep his balance, he struck the asphalt in waves, elbows and chest first, then jaw and eye socket in a stunning jolt that bounced his head as if his neck were a spring. Instinct told him to rise, but his assailant's knee dropped like a dumbbell between his shoulder blades and he flattened, lying still even as his wallet was jerked from his back pocket. Much later he managed to push himself upward into a pained, unsteady crouch, and then to a cautious posture he thought of as vertical. When he reached to check the empty pocket, his hand grasped only a thready remnant of cloth, which he let flutter to the ground.

The journey to the hotel entrance seemed immeasurable now, his face burning and throbbing at the same time. When he finally arrived at the front door he leaned his weight against the glass and stumbled inward, only to see the front desk again unoccupied. Halted, he wondered whether his aching jaw was broken, whether he could call for help with anything resembling human sound.

From his right appeared a man in soiled blue, face blurred beneath a red cap until the face shaped itself into a likeness Ray knew. "I got you, Bud," Trace was saying. "Let's just slide over to this chair." Ray felt strong arms guiding him, lowering him to cushioned fabric, and when he leaned back, his head cradled comfortably in the corner of a wing chair. He let his eyes close.

"What happened to you, man? Stay awake now."

Ray willed his eyelids open. He saw Trace had shoved the cap high on his shining head. "Bastard robbed me," he mumbled, and felt something wet leak from his mouth.

Trace drove him to the hospital in the loaner from the insurance company, and by the time they arrived Ray's swimmy head had begun to clear. His insurance card was lost with his wallet, but the emergency room staff bandaged his scrapes and checked him for concussion syndrome. After a couple of hours under observation he was released, and Trace led him out onto the well-lit parking lot. Ray still felt jumpy at the hint of any shadow and was thankful for another body at his side. Only then did he think to ask why Trace had returned to the hotel.

"Just thought I should check on you," he said. "Make sure you had a way back tomorrow."

A low breeze scraped an empty Doritos bag across their path, and Ray suddenly realized he'd made no arrangements beyond the interview. He wasn't even sure he wanted to go through with it now. "I've got no plans," he said. "The ones I had look shot to hell."

Trace opened the passenger side door and held it for him while Ray folded in one sore limb at a time. As they left the parking lot and merged into traffic, Ray studied Trace's profile, considered how long the man's day had been. "You're heading home tonight, I guess?"

Trace shrugged. "I could probably find a room somewhere, stay over till after your thing tomorrow. Stan owes me some time."

Ray's mood turned a deeper blue, and he wondered what might move him to make the same offer to a stranger, even someone closer. He recalled an incident last fall when he'd let Teresa fend for herself after a water pipe had broken in the basement and he didn't want to run out on a meeting with the chancellor. She'd barely spoken to him for a week after that, leaving his dinners on the stove and keeping her distance as if one touch from his hand might scald her skin. The memory turned something in his stomach, and by the time the Fairmont marquee came into sight he realized he could summon no energy for tomorrow's interview. Perhaps if Western allowed him to re-schedule he could kindle his enthusiasm again, but he doubted it. "No need to wait on me," he said. "I'll go whenever you're ready."

They parked near the entrance, and Ray could feel Trace's steady gaze. "You sure? What about needing a change and all that?"

Ray shifted painfully in his seat. "I do," he said. "But this isn't the place for it."

Trace lifted the cap and raked fingers through what was left of his hair. "I can hear that," he said. "You want to leave now?"

Ray thought about the call he would need to make to Teresa, how he'd have to tell her about the car, and being robbed, even ask her to drive a hundred miles through the dark to Ajax. For a moment his chest constricted, but then he realized she would go to such lengths for him, even tonight. He swallowed and turned his face to the glass. "Just let me have a couple of minutes," he told Trace. "Then I'll be ready to go home."

First appeared in *Hard Toward Home* from Press 53, 2016

Kelli Allen

Between Your Hand and Some Answer

There was ice in the river last night, floes
blue in a double blossom against current,
under hanging willow branches. I am in love

with this gathering and when you looked
at your hand in its accidental brush near
my shoulder, I remembered first to tell you
about the frozen crowning, the way ice became, for
me, a world of praise, but the words stopped,
smoked out and away, disheveled intent, and instead

I let you touch me again, deliberate, and in some stupor
agreed that the night could be colder, that we, too, could
burn longer if we leaned closer to the tree's rough bark.

We arrived identically with our backs pressed,
a confluence, and there was nothing in that bourbon bottle
that could lessen what I heard you say, your wooden
horse all at once the color of some midnight sun.

Laura Baird

Moving

I think I've got it, this moving towards you
until the conversation we make as evening falls
is a mystery. I'm on one side of the table eating
macadamia nuts, sipping black tea, you're
sitting across from me working. Neither of us
speaking. Reality's snapshots.
Comparing moments every now and then, all
of it, a long shot. So, when you asked me
to help pack your things from the bedroom
closet, and I found a dusty box of nude pictures
of your wife, dead four years now, you said,
close your eyes, taking the box, there's no need
to pack these and tossing them out with the avocado seed,
egg shells, and coffee grinds from our Paleo breakfast.
Neither of us spoke about the pictures, listening
instead to the rhythmic flick-hiss of summer sprinklers.
I thought we could open boxes of photographs,
and save only memories we want to keep.
We'll just slip the traces, like the light visiting
earth, across time zones from space, all electrical
impulses that can now be harnessed to make
individual brain cells blink on cue like tiny
Christmas lights. It isn't like that. Each day,
seeks its insider access, and we aren't born
into any present, we penetrate it, failing,
and attempting a translation of our separateness,
kneading the complexities, helping to hide fault,
where all that is good for the heart wakes,
and our histories are a series of calculated risks
moving, like the iron rushing through my blood
that began as stars trillions of miles away.

Ian Bodkin

Consume

In Missouri, I dreamt last night about a friend,
who'd gained a hundred pounds, that or a field

of wild strawberries just south of Kansas City,
which reminds me of the snake-berries that used

to litter our backyard. What could have been sweet
and delicious on hot days of mowing, *oh look upon*

the red push-mower glazed in dew beside the…nope, that's
poison and I used to imagine zoot suited serpents

in white fedoras slithering through the yard at night
just to plant their seed. But that was in Virginia,

where we had chickens once, until they broke out of
the coop and attacked our ducks, which didn't do

anything. To this day there are still rumors of a wild
band of chickens roaming the mountainside stealing

the feed of other small foul and sometimes in the
early light you can hear the lone, feral and far off cry

of cockle-doodle-do! Like my friend who gained so
much weight, I am not in the Blue Ridge anymore,

but further south from the beginning, nestled
between the sheer faces of the Ozarks standing

above a river where even with the added weight, my
friend looks pretty, pretty for here, with a Keystone

in his hand, a Superman snapback with its creased
brim pushed back on his flat black hair. I asked him

once if he wanted a beard in this poem, but he just
twisted his lip to one corner of his mouth and shook

his head because he really wanted to tell me about
a woman in New York City who was arrested for

misusing a roll of Jimmy Dean sausage on a subway.
It all makes me think of salsa, salsa for one. I can

understand how the food can be confused for
a lover. Or maybe I got it wrong and that is the

perverse nature of my society. Maybe the sausage
was only a friend, quivering, in the dream or a quiet

stop as she rustled the plastic bag searching for her
roll of premium pork sausage because of Sundays

and she's from Texas and her father used to make
a cure for his hangover, an apology to her mother,

the sizzle and crackle as the morning light came,
keeping his hands busy and his mouth shut, but I

devour it. Projecting my own dim thoughts, the way
I scream in public—the wild of humanity—and there

on a platform in the dark on a mountain by a river
I want the world to know. For me, love is a full belly.

Nikki Boss

Impossible

IT STARTED SLOWLY -- a drunken comment here, a lingering glance there. They both wanted it to happen in their minds and got too close in the flesh. It was one of those nights, too many drinks around a backyard campfire and then there was music and the girl was giving the boy a lap dance.

"I always knew this would happen." She slipped a leg through his knees, leaning her hips towards him. The fire flickered lower behind them. "Did you?" He kissed her then. He wanted to kiss her. She was too similar to him, this girl, always ready to party.

"You knew it would happen. Did you want it to?" she smiled.

He chose not to answer. His response was to lie her down, screwing her there in the grass while his wife slept on, oblivious, in the house.

They almost got caught the first time but were excellent liars. So they stayed away from one another until they met at a bar and stayed out too late, screwing in his truck and running the battery down.

It went on for a few more weeks, more than a fling and almost an affair, but then it had to stop. He was too afraid of getting caught. Besides, she was everything he never wanted, always smoking a cigarette and covered in tattoos. It was simply an impossible sort of thing to carry on.

He was young when he got married. His wife should have stayed his girlfriend but by then the kids existed; it was too late to leave. He could not leave his wife and kids.

No matter how enticing someone else may be.

No matter that they collide perfectly despite (or perhaps in spite of) their destructive behavior.

Maybe the two of them exist in a parallel world.

He holds his wife at night but looks through her, to the sheets where he still sees her writhing underneath him.

Michael Brasier

Falling Through the Cracks

The Greyhound bus is malnourished, with few passengers unevenly spaced in the seats. I'm hidden in the back, thumbing through the list of albums on my IPod. The squeals of ancient brake pads are shrill even with the buds in my ears. I press play. "Mother's Little Helper" by the Stones.

The bus passes through familiar neighborhoods. I sink further, hoping to disappear into the crack of the seat. The bus screeches to a halt at Main and Elm. There's the Radio Shack. Three kids skate up and down the sidewalk in front of the building. Two others play hacky sack, a game commonplace from my childhood.

An old man gets on the bus. Sleeveless shirt, paint stained jeans, Bass Pro hat, and rolled up newspaper hanging from one of his pockets. He shuffles to the back. I hope he doesn't sit near me, but I'm a fool.

"You from out of town?" he asks.

I nod.

"What brings you here?"

"Uncle passed away," I say.

He apologizes and leaves me alone.

It is late summer, the air simmering much like the day of my mother's funeral. Sweat seeps through my clothes and beads drip from my beard. I wonder what my family would think of the new facial hair. They've only seen early pictures of the growth. I exit the bus a few blocks from my destination and ease down the sidewalk.

It isn't much of a sight, Aunt Darlene's two story house. The off-white paint has been replaced with sky blue coating, and there is a new rock pathway to the house. I see a curtain move in a window.

Darlene's voice yells from inside the house. "Where've you been, hun?"

When my mother passed away, soon after my father did, Darlene went out of her way to make sure I had lunch money. Until I started tenth grade, she'd pick me up from school. She doesn't bother grabbing a coat on her way out, the cold weather the last thing on her mind. She has pronounced crow's feet and her hair looks like a blend of coffee and milk. Aunt Darlene embraces me. I haven't been hugged in years.

Karen Burton

In Fourteen Seconds

1

The hickory nut falls, a single plop as the river swallows;
she exhales smoke from her corner mouth, "I could never live
    in the city."
Ashes fall onto the surface, minnows darting into submerged
smoke formations, away from toes venturing underwater.

An oak leaf floats by, absorbing moisture, beginning its
journey sinking into the riverbed, a vagrant's graveyard.
The current massages the stones below, histories consumed,
erasing ridges earned through tumbles and expansion.

The riverbank lies raw and exposed, soil stroked away,
tree roots curled like snakes waiting to strike.
The purple spiderworts line the bank, audience to erosion,
swaying in freedom from the water's reach.

Once a twig, a melting pile of algae and rot feeds
tadpoles feasting to grow land legs.
Their ancestors croak warnings from the safe soil, unheeded
amongst siren songs of cascading water.

She inhales the reptile aroma, tobacco smoke, smiling
from her corner mouth, "The city is too cruel, ya
know?" The water flows over her feet, carressing
even as minnows return to nibble her dying skin.

2

Boiling river roars,
chews, crunching trees.
Splitting wood groans
discordant melody.
Metal screams,
forced into grotesque sculptures.

She watches--horrified,
delighted.
Cow carcasses pop into
air as muddy mouths
suck and spit, leeching
blood, freakish crimson
swirls.

White box bobbles
like cork twirling, macabre
ballet, raised red flag,
known name displayed, postage lost.
Grave marker,
floating in root-shingle flora.

Knees folding,
she watches
toothy waters
chew the sodden levee.

3

She wakes to lapping water music.
She smiles; she stretches.
Childhood dreams fog her vision--
shoddy rafts dumping explorers
into chilly swirls,
spring-fed, never warm.

Cold wet fingers brush her
hand. The raft has failed, again!
She plunges into freezing pools,
falling awake to dark invasion.
Breaking glass chimes;
hungry currents dine.

She swims to stairs now sodden,
the current pressing rails into her back.
She crawls; she climbs.
Children sleep above, river bank
picnics fill their dreams.

The water ceases climbing,
its belly full of pots and curtains.
She grabs the rail, rising above the churn.
She reaches out, claiming the silver
frame afloat at her feet.

Natalie Byers

King of Center Creek

in ripped overalls, flannel, and
hunting camo, a beard to make Moses
jealous. In Brooklyn, you'd be
fashionable you'd be an artist.
        Famous even. But
here you don't give a fuck.
Here, in the Ozarks
you are King of Cinner Crik
and all its sacred cows.
You rule with a muddy fist and
scream with the feral dogs
to warm yourself in a blizzard.
        You're my first pick
for the zombie apocalypse; my sweetheart
smoking blunts on dirt roads going
next to ninety on E, no GPS, no way back but
we're breaking speakers with
Snoop and Dre. White on Sunday. Hallelujah. Not amen.
King, you're my good luck Big Poppa charm
holding me in our hometown bowling alley bar
while you play wing man for the oil rigger I leave with.
Spend the night in a candy red Jeep with, but never call back.
Nah. I just want ole Center
        Creek to take me home,
slow, windows down. *How many county lines you think*
we can cross on gravel roads? Six.
We cruise through Pierce City (post-tornado, half-re-
built) and back around Polaski Cemetery. You're telling
me how the frogs bellow when they're
full of seed and the kayotes

sing when they're lonely. Teaching me pumpkin shootin' and beer swillin'. Pointing out ankles and clavicles and hip bones. *Those are the sweet spots, you tell me. Those are the spots that matter.*

Richard Jackson Writes About Love and Traps Robert Vivian in a Poem

Pain is a window to freedom.

Winter in Vermont interrupts our
        space. The words we
                can't say are in there.

JACK: Do not sabotage me. If you
want to be a lightweight, that's your
call. But do not sabotage me. And if
they want to drink Merlot, we're drinking Merlot.
MILES: *(dead serious)* If anyone orders
Merlot, I'm leaving. I am not drinking
any fucking Merlot!

As a young artist, Marina Abramović endured countless physically demanding performances. She cut a star around her navel. Whipped herself. For hours. Weeks. Until she was free from fear; until she liberated herself from the experience.

Snow is blinding
        and magnificent. The
                way watching a naked

woman running into
        a wall over and over
                might feel. Somehow,
the terror of it all
        makes sense. Makes
                everything make sense.

If you can control pain in the body, you can control the mind.

Merlot grapes are a hearty, sweet varietal that are easily massed produced into flat wines with no character. Most forgettable wines are heavily based on Merlot.

When I'm sad, I read love
        poems by Rick Jackson
                because they're not really

about love, not *that* kind
        of love. But *love*. It's love like
                Bob dancing a New Year's

Eve high knee Riverdance
        with arms in position
                one. It reminds me

of that good ache found in
        Vermont snow. Great
                and terrible snow.

Marcus Cafagña

The Law of Gravity

Strolling down the gallery
of cells, a bemused guard

hands me hot coffee,
but with the sugar spilled

along the seam of the cup
my fingers feel the burn.

And there's no one to thank
for the seven hundred miles

I hitchhiked from Ann Arbor
only to be caught trespassing

in an underground Car-Park
in Boston, for the free trip

to jail. A conga line of
cockroaches stretch

down to my commode
from the tier of cells

on the floor above,
where I can hear a door

roll shut and someone
in the drunk tank, crying.

Under my wall-mounted bunk,
I uncover a pair of old pants,

shoes, eyeglasses—
signs I might be lucky,

that the man here before me
has died or walked out naked.

First appeared in *Long Shot*

Katch Campbell

Written in the Book of Life

There were no muses on the night of my birth. Heaven was on vacation and Hell was hosting a dervish. Does anyone else wonder why we look both ways during REM sleep? I am looking for a bigger story—something to suggest my Libra status instead of this history-less offering of a title. What is the value of a name and how much time should be given? I spent an hour writing his name over and over in ink. Four hundred and thirty-six times in block letters. That's just over seven times a minute and not one of them conjured him any closer than this page. I am still wondering if it was a mistake to break it off. My head says cleave and my heart does too. I'm not a fan of the two way street though who advocates adventure down a dead end? Were we of Science or Passion? This morning someone said when a person is moved by art they have understood it. Here is what I remember of our last night: his hands on my spine after peeling oranges, my nose trailing the sweat lines of his muscle, how the light from the river coated our sex in purple, and the silver clippings from his head in the sink. One must acknowledge there will be no contract with God or his agents of justice.

Barbara Siegel Carlson

The Pear

I love to say *angel hair,* imagining the soft
light body of a god slipping down my throat.
A divine hum on my tongue, a slight thing, a
sensation. Pessoa wrote that he loved such
fruitless things as they open a humble stasis
in our lives. Maybe that's why I keep
the petrified pear on my windowsill.
This shrunken wooden knob that collects dust
is a mystery once juicy with seeds and dangling
from a tree behind a wall. I found it
in my friend's yard in Romania.
My friend survived terrible times in her country,
standing in line all day for a lump of butter,
overwhelmed by caring for orphans left in cribs,
inconsolable whose eyes looked too large
inside their dark circles. They would
only shiver a little under thin covers,
as though they had thickened their own skin. But
sometimes she would hear their high-pitched cries
ringing down the hall, softer and softer,
only at night they rose in waves
through the water-stained walls of her dreams.
The heart can shrivel like fruit never picked, or
soften with water that never stops running,
rising now over sea walls. And this fruit, this pear
perhaps withered on the sooty tree in her yard and
filled with rain before dropping to the ground.
It didn't fester like the sores of the dogs
that roamed the streets, growling at every turn.
Maybe it's futile to speak about the mystery

of what happens inside or ever understand the
plight of another. Or take life like a vulture
that eats out the heart. I must tell how my friend lived
for a year on a pig she had butchered, gnawing
on every bone, sucking the marrow juice out
before the freezer went dead, and the stench
seemed to speak for itself. Even the dogs
whimpered past. Somehow the tree grew
in the dirt and the stink, the roots pushing deep,
and still the dew glistened on the hanging
and the fallen. Last winter she sat by her wall, petrified
as people passed on the other side, her stomach
growing hard with cancer. By then she could eat only
the softest things. Not one of her pears
sliced with a butter knife could save her.
Maybe we say a few words, however slight,
to soften the terror that our soul will be swallowed
by the silence of the body, the pear waiting to be plucked
before melting to earth with its endless grip.

KITTY CARPENTER

Between Silences

       the sounding of a whippoorwill carries
across the browning field,
       bullfrogs are slicking through the
black Missouri mud. My nails itch,
       the earth beneath them drying
after patting down a small grave
       scooped out for a fallen fledgling.
A moccasin slips past me into the murky
       water as I kneel
to rinse my hands, his dark body
       a venomous ribbon.
I draw back, though
       it is not fear which moves me.

Between silences
       long fingers of shadow brush my shoulders;
the first star materializes;
       I know I am neither earth, nor star—
though closer now to this dark earth,
       a million of which could be swallowed
into the steady sun—its bright burn still less
       than a rogue electron
next to Antares's cosmic blaze
       and yet as a quail softly calls,
I answer into the static air
       and he hears,
calls back again.

Derek Cowsert

Fire Places

IN THE SUMMER OF 2005, between Yuma and San Diego, I looked out the duct-taped window of my beater '94 Accord and saw what seemed to be miles of flames, maybe two stories high, a few hundred yards from the freeway.

"That look like a controlled burn to you?" I asked my buddy Eric.

He perked up, looked out. "Gotta be."

Eric had grown up in San Diego, so I figured he'd know. My third year of college, he had been my pudgy, nerdy, freshman neighbor in the dorms when I was a junior looking to show off my campus acumen. I took him under my wing and made him my intern at the college radio station. He made professional-sounding radio drops for our show and gave me someone to converse with about music on the air between songs. When I disappeared on a coke bender later that year, he took over the radio show without missing a beat.

Eric helped me seem more official, and in turn, I helped him seem cooler. In college, I carried myself with a false bravado that came across as cool, and a lot of people bought it, even if deep down it wasn't true. He was my first choice when I needed a co-pilot for my cross-country road trip. Months earlier, I'd convinced him to reroute his flight back from his semester in Edinburgh to meet me in upstate New York and see the country from the open road rather than the sky.

"You ever fix your brakes?" he asked me when I picked him up at the Albany airport.

"They work."

We drove back to Saratoga Springs to pack and secure all the supplies – two ounces of high quality marijuana, a family-size container of off-brand peanut butter I'd infused with an ounce of lower quality pot, and 100 hits of heavy blotter acid mailed to me from a friend in San Francisco. I also had to say goodbye to my girlfriend.

We'd met at USC, only to have her father pull her out of school and move her all the way across the country just to get her away from me. I loved that girl. At least I thought I did. After my graduation, I had followed her to New York. I stayed for a year, until we both agreed I had to go back to California and get a real job doing something with my film degree in Hollywood. All I had left of her on that road trip with Eric was the iPod she got me for my 22nd birthday and my tee-shirt, stained with her mascara in the shape of two ash colored spots.

Eric and I went sightseeing in New York City before heading to Cincinnati for a night, and then detoured north to Michigan. I veered off course for Eric, who was still a virgin at the age of 21 and quite self-conscious over it. There was a girl he knew from high school taking summer classes in Michigan, ready and willing to cure him of his innocence. We stopped off at her dorm suite and played some drinking games before she and Eric left me to watch television in her living room with the sound way up.

Eric and I left after breakfast the next day, me with a neck stiff from couch sleeping and him freshly mitzvahed. We weren't even in out of the parking lot before Eric told me "I like-ah her boobies," and I fell out.

"Don't ever say I wasn't there for you, bro," I told him. "Now pack a bowl and let's hit the highway."

On our way west, we crashed with family and friends in Chicago, southern Indiana, southwest Missouri, Houston, the Grand Canyon, and rural Arizona, dropping acid and ecstasy, smoking our lungs like briskets, drinking our livers to the brink, puking, passing out, waking up and driving to the next town to do more of the same. By the final leg of our trip, we were incoherent, barely cognizant of our surroundings. We needed to sleep and eat and detox, but first we had to drive a little further.

Eric nestled his head back inside the crook of his elbow against the passenger door. I watched the flames through my windows and mirrors. When we got to Eric's parents' house – a one-story adobe on a cul de sac in the San Diego suburb of Poway – he and I were both exhausted. We slid out of my car ready for bed. Eric's parents met us outside. They asked about the trip and the drive. They wanted to know how things had gone with Eric's aunt in Yuma. Mostly, though, they asked us about the fire.

"Did you see it?" Eric's mom asked.

Eric's parents were middle-aged and out of shape, with loose clothes and lots of love to give. His dad drove for UPS. His mom didn't work.

"See what?" Eric asked between hugs.

"The fire. You boys get close enough to see the smoke or anything?" His dad asked.

"The controlled burn?" I grabbed some bags from the trunk.

"That wasn't a burn. Don't you boys listen to the radio?" His mom smiled in our direction, cloudy eyes open.

"No shit, really? We were right in the middle of it." Eric said. His father led us into the house, where a floppy long-haired dog nuzzled into my leg at the door.

"That's my seeing eye dog. Or at least, he used to be. He went blind," Eric's mother told me.

The dog's eyes were like hers, smoky and glazed over. I knelt to pet him and thought about how I'd been oblivious to the surrounding danger and destruction of the fire we'd just driven through. It's been that way with me and fire all my life, or at least as long as I remember. I seem to always find myself around fire, or maybe it finds me.

The first fire I remember from my childhood spread its controlled warmth and heat from the wood-burning stove in the living room of my family's first home, a red brick house near the top of a hill I used to love to ride my bike down. That fire burned out of sight behind the door of a small, black, cast-iron fortress we children were told never to touch, but I'd put my hand to it when no one was looking, just for a second, just to feel the sizzle on my fingertip.

I spent quiet moments out back of that house, collecting seed pod spinners dropped from the oak tree onto the wooden floors and railings of the porch above the carport. Some days, after brutal mockings at school, I'd come home and stand out on that porch and drop spinner after spinner, watching them flutter to the ground and wondering what was wrong with me.

I found out recently the red brick exterior of that house wasn't brick at all. It was a red faux-brick siding that caused massive headaches for my parents, both in trying to insure the house, and later when they tried to sell it. The siding, it turns out, was highly flammable.

*

After three days' rest at Eric's parents' house, I found the strength to head north to Los Angeles. All my friends were there, along with what few work opportunities I had. Many of my best friends were still in school and living together in a large rental home we called The Pirate House, so named because of the Jolly Roger flag flown from the house's peak. I crashed there for awhile.

For Christmas that year, we filled nine keg shells with cheap beer, bought dozens of sets of white icicle lights, rented a snow machine, and created a real life winter wonderland in the front yard, two blocks from the USC campus. Earlier in the day, the house came into possession of three cases of Energy Fuel, a non-FDA approved energy drink some students were promoting. They were supposed to promote their product at a frat that night, but when that party got canceled, they gave us all their product for free if we let them "sponsor" our party, which only meant allowing them to hang a banner off the front porch. The Energy Fuel got mixed into the jungle juice, which got mixed into hundreds of guests, many of whom got blackout drunk and tried to hook up all over the house. We ended the party and kicked everyone out when we caught a couple fucking in the living room.

The residents and regulars went out the next night. I stayed behind on the couch. They returned home long after midnight and kept the party going by mixing what was left of the Energy Fuel with what was left of the keg beer. Someone threw a folding chair off the porch and onto the lawn, and that set off a chain reaction. Another chair, then another. Then the recliner. Then the couch. The whole group drunk on beer and that awful energy poison, somebody took a lighter to the errant sprigs of fluff coming out of the couch cushions. The couch went up faster than anyone expected.

I slept through the whole ordeal. When I stepped out to smoke a cigarette the next morning, I saw the rubble. What remained of the couch, frame and springs mostly, along with chunks of chairs and metal hinges of the recliner, all charred, burned gray and black, sitting atop a pile of ashes on grassless patch of blackened yard. It looked to me like a chaotic version of the fire pit my grandpa and dad taught me to set up in the deer woods when I was a teenager.

My first deer season in the woods in rural Missouri, we set up in tents around a fire pit. Our latrine was a chair with a hole cut in the center placed over a hole dug in the ground inside an extra tent. I felt like we were really roughing it.

My family considered fourteen plenty old enough to handle a gun, and they tried to get me to hunt, but it didn't take. I had no interest in killing an animal, and furthermore I was a terrible shot. Firing a weapon didn't make me feel like a man. Building the fire did. I loved the primal aspect of it. I imagined myself a woodsman, a caveman, a pioneer. I enjoyed the feel of the ax in my hand, the smooth curve of the handle, the heft and power of the thick, metal blade. My father's ax became an extension of me and gave my skinny arms a strength they'd never known.

I left my elders to their cold, damp mornings in their tree-stands. In lieu of hunting, I took charge of the campfire. I felled slender trees – only hardwoods, no pine or cedar – with a long downward slanting chop followed by a straight-ahead cut near the trunk. Each time a tree hit the ground, I smiled to myself as I set to work snapping off the branches, saving them for kindling. I used my foot to steady these trees as I cut them into smaller logs and carried them to the campsite myself. I tended the fire all day and night.

Once I had the technique down, I refused any help. The fire was my responsibility. I was proud of it. I made and controlled it. The fire was a necessity. It kept us warm. The fire gave me a purpose, and I tended it with vigilance. Out there in those woods, away from the world and all my issues, I felt a kinship with that fire, though I wouldn't understand why until I was much older.

*

Eric pulled me out of L.A. in 2007 to write for his Internet start-up down in San Diego. I moved in with him and his childhood buddy, Steve, all of us burning through investor money while we tried to get a website off the ground. Our original apartment in Poway was a shitty three-bedroom just off the freeway. We did our best to make it look decent by hanging some posters and mirrors, but the furniture didn't match and the carpet never stayed clean. Our crown jewel was a whiteboard on the wall in the dining room where we wrote ideas for fake band names, for no other reason than because it amused us: MC Threenis and the Foreskins, Steve McQueen's Psychedelic Wet

Dream, Scrotallica, Antiquated Porn Machine, that kind of thing. We played at being professional grown-up adults, but really we were just stupid kids.

One day that summer, Eric bought a 60-inch flatscreen from Best Buy, straight cash. That October, his massive TV showed the flames of the San Diego wildfires in high definition as we watched them burn through houses one town over in Rancho Bernardo. The fire was on every channel. Qualcomm Stadium – San Diego's pro football venue – opened its doors to refugees as the fires multiplied, jumped freeways and closed in around us. Surrounded by the fire, watching it burn through homes only a few miles from us, I begged the guys to leave for Qualcomm.

"The stadium is for the displaced," Steve told me.

"And what the fuck would you call us?" I asked.

"We're fine. We're still in the Green Zone," Eric said.

Their assurances did nothing to calm me. The idea of staying and waiting struck me as preposterous. We watched whole houses and neighborhoods burn down on the big screen and charted the fire's encroachment from every direction via online mapping services, like an approaching storm on radar.

I almost had Steve and Eric convinced to head to the stadium when our drug dealer, Logan, showed up. "My mom is flipping out over this fire shit. Can I stay with you guys?" he asked as he dropped his backpack on our coffee table. "I got an ounce of pot and an eight ball."

With that, I was overruled. We made a run to the corner convenience store and bought four Heineken mini-kegs and a carton of smokes. Then we went back to the apartment to hunker down.

Logan didn't normally deal in cocaine. What he had that night looked strange to me. Nothing like the stuff I'd done in the past. It had this shine to it, like nail polish, like somebody cut it with lacquer. I did some anyway, and every line burned my nostrils. I beat the leaving drum for another hour or so, but the guys convinced me we'd be fine. Logan rolled a blunt for us to smoke to calm my nerves, and I did a couple more lines and chugged a pint of beer to lift my spirits. Steve stayed sober, just in case we really did need to evacuate to the stadium. It took a few hours of beers, lines, and bong rips, but as the sun set I felt less freaked out.

By the evening, the blaze had become so passé to my friends that they switched out the news cycle for video games. I kept racking lines and downing beer and watching the fire's progress on my laptop, charting its proximity to our apartment, staying vigilant in case we needed to evacuate the complex. By 2 A.M., it was just me and the remnants of the eight-ball, still piled like incandescent ash on the table. I rolled myself a joint, did two more lines, and poured another beer to take onto the porch.

I was half through the joint when the fire crested the hill about a mile east of our Poway apartment complex. At first I couldn't tell what I was looking at—just a red line, snaking, stretching, coming for me. I stared at it until I realized what it was. The fire crept closer. I wanted to wake everyone, drag them out of bed, and get us all to the safe zone, but I remained silent. For fear of being mocked for cowardice, I didn't warn my friends of the danger close-at-hand.

I stood outside and smoked. The cocaine was doing less and less for me, each line keeping me high not quite as long as the last one. I was drunk, drowsy and morose, starting on the descending limb of a cocaine comedown. I thought about my family, what they'd think of me in that moment, on another fucking bender.

I finished the joint, went inside, washed down a couple of my sleeping pills with the rest of my beer, snorted the last of the shimmering coke on the table in one fat line, and crawled into bed. I didn't wake anybody that night because I wanted the fire to come and take me.

Eric pounded on my door the next morning. "Yo dude, you awake in there?"

"Yeah." I coughed. "I'm up. Time is it?
"Like eight-thirty, man. You got work today?"

"We should go check out the town," Logan shouted from the bathroom as I opened my door.

I didn't have work, and neither did anyone else. The whole city and surrounding suburbs took that Friday off, so the four of us crammed into Eric's car and set out to take stock of the wreckage. Felled trees. Blackened houses. Ashen chunks of buildings. Half of Poway High School, gone. Thick brown smoke hung like grimy fog at street level. Rain, ice, floods, wind – none destroy like fire. Fire eats. That's how the houses looked to me. Eaten. Gnawed on like a demon's chew toy. We drove down the road where some friends of Logan's lived and saw entire roads wiped out, save for the frames of a few houses, all the insides charred and visible.

I kept quiet, minding my own problems, thinking about that morning, when I'd woken up an hour or so before everyone else. My first inclination was to check the progress of the fire, but when I rolled over to hit the snooze button on my phone alarm, my cheek stuck to the pillow. I rose to find a crusty maroon stain where I'd slept. Confused and hung-over, I stumbled to the bathroom and looked at myself in the mirror. At first I couldn't tell what I was looking at. Just a red line snaking, stretching, coming for me. I stared at it until I realized what it was. Dried blood, leaking out of nose while I slept.

Eventually we headed back to the apartment and kept drinking. Once we were home and I was good and fucked up again, I told the guys about my morning. We had a laugh about it, about what a crazy asshole I was, about how I picked the night we had fire blowing in from every side to blow enough of that lustrous coke to give me nosebleed, about how I was sure to die soon if I didn't slow it down. Everything was a joke back then. I danced among the consequences, avoided all the worst ones, and wondered what the fuck was wrong with me.

*

When the lease in Poway ran out, Kevin, Eric and I moved into a fancy three-bedroom duplex in Mission Valley, in the center of San Diego proper. Our 2008 Halloween party came together at the last minute. Logan's community college water polo teammates needed a place to party, so they invited the volleyball players, girls swim team, and cheerleaders to our place. I had no costume, so I settled on just walking around in my boxers and a button-up with dress socks and shouting, "I'm not wearing any pants!"

The party drew maybe one hundred people or so. We had beer pong going in two different rooms, plus a living room dance party. Some of the water polo guys showed their gratitude for the use of our home as their party venue via hourly taps on the shoulder and trips to the upstairs bathroom to snort their cocaine, free of charge.

Late in the night, three girls showed up, all them dressed in matching Tom Cruise *Risky Business* costumes, right down to the whitey tighties. One of them spotted me in the kitchen pouring a drink.

"We match!" She leaned hard into me.

"Yeah, totally."

"Do you have a place I can put my bag?" she asked, holding up one of those backpack-sized leather purses with the smooth, curved wooden handles. She was brunette. Cute. Maybe 20 years old, tops. Her nose was red and dry. Her eyes were all lit up.

"I mean, there's my room, but it's upstairs."

She hooked her arm into mine. "Show me."

Upstairs, in my room, this girl whose name I never got dumped the contents of a coke baggie onto my bedside table and asked me, "So you party, right?"

She was cutting two lines when the fire alarms blared in the apartment and outside. Figuring the pot smoke in our apartment had triggered the system and the cops would be arriving soon, I shuffled the brunette out of my room, but not before we snorted and gummed what she'd racked up.

Downstairs, the crowd stood awaiting instruction. I inspected every room of the first floor, and once I was convinced the fire wasn't our fault, I stepped out into our complex's courtyard, pantsless. Many other tenants, all fully clothed, some holding children, stood outside their doors as well. They looked from me to the flashing lights of our apartment-wide fire alarm system. I saw no smoke. I smelled nothing. I went back inside.

"Everybody out of the building!" I announced. "Something's on fire somewhere!"

Despite, or perhaps because of, the sirens and flashing lights up and down our street, the guests dispersed quickly. They got in their cars and drove home drunk and stoned and coked to the gills. The threat of fire scares people. It drives people away.

*

When I lost my job in 2009, Eric and Logan kicked me out of the apartment. Once I couldn't pay my share for rent, drugs, or booze, they didn't have much use for me. I sold what I couldn't pack in suitcases and boxes and load into my car, found someone to take my room, and left San Diego. I heard from Eric one more time, when he called to tell me he and Logan kicked out my replacement and expected me to send them rent money. When I refused, he cursed me up and down. That's the last time we spoke. Just getting fucked up with a guy ain't a great base for lifelong friendship. No amount of near-death experiences and getting a guy laid can change that fact.

For a few weeks I crashed in L.A. with a college buddy – a poet and fellow addict. We slept on dual twin beds, L-shaped along two walls in his one bedroom artist's hovel, drinking breakfast to bedtime, me spending my severance money on booze and drugs. I tried to get another job, but I was wrecked and the economy was in shambles. My parents offered to buy me a ticket back to Missouri, on the condition that I sober up and attend weekly meetings at a local twelve step program. I accepted their offer was because I was afraid I'd die in that apartment if I didn't.

At age 26, I checked out my first twelve-step meeting. I got a sponsor. I read the AA big book and worked the steps. That whole deal, I gave it a real shot. My sponsor was the first person I told almost everything. He heard more about my life – the drugs, the pain, the fires – than anyone up to that point. I didn't miss a meeting, every Friday night, in the sanctuary of my father's church.

That first sober winter, I'd huddle with my family around the stone fireplace in the living room, spending mornings and evenings, sipping coffee under blankets, eating homemade chocolate chip cookies, the warmth of the burning hickory drawing us together. I loved that fire. I loved smelling the wood, stoking the embers and turning the logs to let the coals breathe, watching the flames grow as they waved and flicked behind the glass doors.

Any time my dad was out working, I'd build the fire. I spent my days that winter perfecting the process. I collected kindling and split hundreds of logs on a stump in our backyard, ax in my hand again, just like in the woods when I was younger. On days when I felt like getting drunk or high so much I trembled, I'd go out and split logs for hours, turn each one into two or three and pile them up under the carport until I exhausted myself, till I couldn't feel my fingers or toes save for the sting of the cold. Then I'd bring some logs inside and feed the fire.

Something in the act of building fire soothes me now. The containment of the fire, watching it burn in an enclosed space, brings a calm over me. The fire is both tame and wild, safe yet dangerous. Like a lion at the zoo.

In a Bible story I was taught as a child, three brothers disobey the king and are cast into a fire as their punishment, but they do not perish. God stands with them inside the fire, the story goes. He protects them from the heat and saves them from the flames. They come out of the fire unscathed. I know this story is fiction because I know fire leaves nothing unscathed. Fire can't help but change everything it touches. That's just how fire's made.

Chris Crabtree

Traveling to Tecumseh, Missouri

The road curves with the contour of the land,
going up over hills and sometimes through
rock walls streaked black by dynamite—
because it's easier to destroy than find
another way— until there is just the one road,
passing rundown middle of nowhere Z highway
homes— scattered toys in the yard, an empty
sandbox, action figures, a big wheel,
next to a rusted swing-set, and some kind
of stove with smoke coming out, and I wonder
what about this land makes people settle?
Maybe it's the beauty of the surroundings that
gives this meaning, or maybe it's the lives
struggling to survive splitting their own
firewood. What else is there?
Only happiness in the experience it seems,
making it easier to accept the seclusion
of the woods, nobody to tell you different,
a reason to get up in the morning,
like a sunrise on the river.

JORDAN CULOTTA

For Kelly

In gratitude, a bundle of roadside wildflowers hung upside-
    down with hemp.

For your wolf-mother heart.

For howling at the moon with me.

For knowing we have not yet heard what we have been
    listening to,
and listening harder in response.

For your vulnerability- the graceful beauty of your naked body
half-dipped in Ozark river water, your back turned to me.

For fixing bacon and eggs for breakfast at your mother's house,
where I wasn't fully welcome to sleep in your bed.

For your uncle's bee's orange-blossomy honey,
which I licked from my fingers on the drive back to Tennessee.

For holding me. For holding me and kneading my ovaries
    with your fist
when I was writhing in tears and feverish.

For looking at the bloody mess I've made
of my heart, and not offering to help me clean it up (this time).

Simply, for your presence-
Even in your absence I feel you here.

For all the things I can't put into words,

because language is all I have,

and yet language is hardly enough;

I've found it takes love to fill an empty cup.

Kristen Cypret

Coping

I found her on the kitchen floor,
    skirt drug up above the knees, ruby-stained fingers
resting on an overturned ashtray.
She raised a half-empty bottle to her lips.
        It teetered along her bottom teeth
    and ribbons of port trickled
down her chin. I wanted to leave her for my dad to
    find in the morning, but this spill
would do more than settle into the carpet so I kneeled
    to grab the bottle. She pulled me into her lap,
her fingers tangled themselves in my hair
    and she caressed my scalp with a Nocturne,
a sorry wrapped in wine burps and heavy pauses.

    I thought she had stopped breathing
        but her voice tickled my ear
and she started singing in her native tongue,
    her words like bourbon tossed back
        on an empty stomach.
For years, I lived with two languages,
    the daughter of a refugee,
a survivor of war but the war never left her. It steeped

    when she glanced in a mirror,
        when a face in the crowd frowned like her sister,
like the boy lynched in Sighetu Marației.

    I wasn't old enough to see
        behind her rouge stained lips,
the smell of another man's cologne rising off her
    skin, but her inebriated chatter dredged

up displaced memories and I leaned back in her arms, hoping to catch one.

JIM DANIELS

Last Day In Coldwater

Our phone died due to lack
of payment. I left her a note
and trudged down gray splintered steps.

She was sleeping the weekly
sleep of the dead,
the morning crash after the stairs
burned down beneath her.

After days of artificially sustained
floating above scorched earth.

Paying bills required
a certain sustained attention.
We had cold water
and nothing more.

Unwritten debts were due.
They had the steepest
interest.

Listening to the blue music
of our veins, we had broken
unwritten rules and red-tagged
our whereabouts.

I walked through dawn and into
hunger, past the smell of coffee
and the shrinking menu
of our young lives.

We were close to Ohio,
closer to Indiana. Michigan
did not want us. We had no friends.
They had exploded

in one of our many miracles gone
wrong. She slept with hands limp
over the fold-out couch—our bed.

She'd want a fix when she awoke
to wind her clock. How many pencils
can you accumulate with dried-out erasers
before you throw them all out?

Disconnected. Perhaps the recorded
message might briefly fool those out
to find us. Precision lost

its wings, then the wheels fell off.
In lieu of fiscal responsibility, we repossessed
each other. The wind swung wide
across the flat land. My face stung

with radioactive love. For her,
for it, and what came first? The drugs. The
drugs came first, so I mention them last.
Someone was going to climb the stairs

and it wouldn't be me, and what
would they demand? I should've
woken her, but I did not. I should've
shaken the map in her face.

Look where we are,
I should have said.

First appeared in *Apology to the Moon*

If You Ever Have To Do This Yourself

My daughter started crying
when she couldn't get the fake poop back
into the fake butt of the Pooping Dog
she won at the school carnival.
She'd squeezed too hard, and the poop popped
out. I was driving home. We'd eaten half-frozen fries
and gristly hot dogs. All for a good cause.

She's in first grade. My son's in third.
His dog still has its poop. She doesn't want me
to say *potty* anymore—too babyish—
yet she was bawling. I lost it, yelling loud enough
to scare us all. Back home, I got them
into bed, my daughter still snuffling, my son
glazed over into silence.

Shamed, I stood in the kitchen jamming
the orange rubber cylinder of poop
back up the plastic dog's butt.
I used index finger, I used thumb,
I used tack hammer. I wet the poop,
then squeezed with needle-nose pliers
until I got it all back in.
Two Pooping Dogs on the counter
for them to find in the morning.
To write their names on in Sharpie marker.

They kissed me when I awoke.
They held their puppies. We have no pets,
though they're always asking.
If you ever have to do this yourself,
keep it together. Shut up
and do love's dirty work.

First appeared in *Apology to the Moon*

CARRIE DIMINO

Missouri to Kansas: The Work Road

The city comes up in pieces—
cathedral, library, newspaper, ballet.
Some mornings the sunrise glitters so gold on
steel it hurts. A thousand concrete pyramids
each with its own lord, each with its own slanting shadow.

The river hails so sudden it's hard to look away
and there is a flood waiting, here, to let go and sing
and a current just under the surface, like the city,
humming to be forgiven or let loose. A murmured
blessing of water, waiting, still, not still.

Then the Bottoms, flat factories and rail yard tracks
sludgy, slung low. They gossip about the slurring night
and the wild dogs, part shade, part glide,
they ramble by princes here.

Across the state line—quieter now green—
the hills come on like mossy waves.
This side of the river banked by nothing but
a solvent fog. A pastoral moment

up in the wood, a doe's still body, an offering
before work. Near the concrete tower crime scene tape flitters
on the roadside, a plea to remember, to be remembered.

Gregory Donovan

Besides

The palominos, sweet doves, gallop here and never
draw any closer. My head hit the rocky wall of the well –
Mister Little To Nothing knocked me in, if you need to
know, my *father*—and that was it. For a while I was thinking
I was thinking, then I wasn't. Like rats in the big barn.
Mouth foam, little beaches. Their vacation paradise.
The grain elevator man told me once rats can laugh.

I died and it wasn't much different from anything else,
maybe it was too much like Nothing's shaky hand
scratching a line through each number on the funeral
home calendar, sending our days into the shit
hole of never never. And where was *what should have been*?
Labor from sunup, no breakfast till noon, beatings
the rest of the day—the neighbors' wild-eyed horses got
treated better, though they got their share of pain.

The last thing in my head, besides *I guess*
it all had to come to this, old daddy of mine
when the hammer landed and I flew,
besides the blue shining all around my shadow
as I spilled into the cold and dark, shimmering
like a starling swooping into the waiting wheel of
light, besides that last glimpsed ripple of cream-gold
waves ruffling the wheat field's hair then the feel of it,
wind on my face I carried with me into the
next world and the next: *Big nothing*
comes from little to nothing you know,
and besides, I'm glad I poisoned the water.

First appeared in *Torn from the Sun*, Red Hen Press

The Grandfather in the Rafters

A form of revenge. Some homegrown Missouri craftsman here
    committed
a bridge. Now it rots under its caved-in, cedar-shingled cover
where once it leapt with a certain grace, windowed, gabled,
    fitted
true as any man's good house, right as rain, clean over

that small island of brush in the raw-banked, often-as-not dry
branch. Where, you said, one summer's day you hid
to watch that goddamn stiff-neck dandy take his ride
through the tall noon. His mare's mane of shining amber

whipping back. His boiled and studded shirtfront,
never stained by anything like sweat. A man ramrod
straight and lordly, until he slowed her to enter— hoof-
clops and wheels rumbling overhead in the lumber—

the shadow in the bridge. In that dark mouth he had been a
thundering brag, a half-minute's worth of hollow promises,
empty threats. And when he came to light again you spit in
your palm. Then smiled. You'd call his bluff.

He went courting every woman a young man might desire
for miles around in that expensive, trim, and pillowed
rig, the black calash top always thrown right back
to show off the seat's tan soft-soaped leathers. Your rough

farm-boy hands were itching for just the trick
a swill-bucket full of slop and black mud might do.
So you sneaked back to climb where you waited, eyes afire
with the framed spark of stars, to throw down that night

a country baptism and burial, a handful of hard words
through gritted teeth: *Here you go, Mister Man: you're dirt, too.*
But he raised up when the horse spooked, and you heard
the thump of his fall making you dead right.

First appeared in *Calling His Children Home*, U. of Missouri Press

Alta Leah Emrick

River Pretty Makeover

Beauty echoed off
The amber-hued trees
Autumn had arrived

Each leaf glistening
With morning fairy dew
Like crystal pellets on a Lily pad

Somewhere among the
Saffron-yellow maples
A lonesome Blue Jay cawed

The river, the liquid soul
Of the woods, roared like
A thousand swishing bubbles

At days end, swooshing water
Lulled us into deepest slumber
Like babes in a rocking cradle

Sentry trees silhouetted the sky
While asterisk stars carved
A marigold harvest moon

Brisk air cleared nostrils and left
Apple-cheek faces; smiling lips
Could not be wiped somber

A potpourri of aromas opened
Our pores and freshened our
Skin with the moisture of nature

Our minds were expanded, filled
And enriched; some makeovers
Are facial and some are cerebral

Brandon Funk

Iambic Cento
> -found by Carrie in a text message

We have arrived.

Nothing much to do at this damp, earthy hour.
It's smooth drinking rye with my brother and father.

Am into the woods again this morning.
How postmodern to text you from hunting.

A misty-fine, dark day, now. Know, I love
cloudy moonshine and you the most.

I slept in this morning, dreaming of Proust.
I've been so damn tired this year. No killing yet.

Back into the woods until dark arrives—
For Christ's sake don't test the knives on skin.

How did you know I've been reading Shakespeare,
in the woods, until dusk? A bit of late sun here.

For now, I shall sleep in the woods. Deep
in the hunt, I forget about pretending.

Anyone good wishes she were in the woods.
Damp still. You haven't yelled at me for days.

D. Gilson

A History of My Father as the History of McDonald's

America on the brink of war, 1940,
and my father born on a dairy farm turned
to dust. In San Bernardino, Dick and Mac
open McDonald's Bar-B-Q, car hop
service and a large menu of fifteen cent single
patties, seventeen with cheese. War Machine.
War spreads. Suburbs bloom. The farm glistens
with Chevrolets and dew, the hum of tractors.
America in need of protein and the demand for
milk. 1949 and potato chips get the axe
for french fries as the dew dries
by milking time, the debut of triple thick
shakes. My father hunts for squirrels
with his brother. *Skeeter shoots 'em straight
between the eyes.* 1955 and the family sells up
for more acreage. High school. The first

drive-thru replete with towering, golden arches,
checkered tile, though by '65 the number
will reach seven hundred. Graduation day,
1959, and my grandmother's forged signature
on enlistment papers. *We will not enter
a conflict in Vietnam.* Dick and Mac build
their hundredth restaurant. Fond Du Lac,
Wisconsin, meaning where the river
is blocked. Lawton, Oklahoma, the year of
our lord and my father's first marriage,
1961. Ray Kroc buys out Dick and Mac
for just under three million. 1963. A daughter.
A Filet-O-Fish is born. McDonald's goes global,

1967. First Puerto Rico then Ottawa as my
father moves his family to the air base in
Okinawa. Big Mac and Hamburglar, reassigned
to Hanoi, 1971, my father, Special Sauce, Agent
Orange, Two All-Beef Atom Bombs. Silence till
'74, stateside in Biloxi. Extramarital maritime
war zone. The Ronald McDonald House opens
its doors. *Carry on my wayward son.*
On the doorstep of Regan, 1979. Divorce.
My mother. First Happy Meals, their plastic
toys. For a brief period, uninterrupted joys.
The Eighties. The McNuggets. The Miscarriage.
Regan re-elected. 1984. Ray Croc passes.
My father leaves. Then comes back. I am born.

Hunter Hobbs

Where I Left My Coat

There used to be a house
here and it was bright and
warm and I had the key
that was before
the door knobs went out of tune
and the milkweed scratched out
its wide-eyed windows
before the swallows choked
on mothballs tucked
under buckling floorboards
I forgot how to read
the street signs
and the snow
has covered my tracks
surely there's a word
for us--something like
desperate--but quieter

Jimmy Huff

Who Cooks for You? Who Cooks for Y'all?

I'VE BEEN HERE BEFORE but still struggle to find the place when I'm looking for it. Hid away; tangles of dirt road unfound and found again. And the river—

The water is riotous at Devil's Elbow, narrow and angry for want of rainfall. But, as always, we have this middle of nowhere river access to ourselves. We unload the canoes, placing them bow first at the water's edge just below the melancholy namesake of this part of the stream—the mighty left turn known to flip the foolhardy. The undertow is too much to compensate for; there's too much going on beneath the surface. You've gotta get out; walk it down—carefully. Or put in here, where we are, fifty yards downstream.

D.D. passes around the inaugural pint of whiskey. "Snake bite medicine," he says. Then we get to it. The day is on.

We meticulously load our canoes full of supplies, all the while wondering what we're forgetting. We are thorough, but time behaves differently at the river. To forget something crucial could be a real shame, not to mention annoying. It only takes one night of sleeping in a chair with a towel for a blanket to truly understand the importance of attention to detail. In the words of Cheech Marin, "Responsibility is a big responsibility, man."

The canoes look ridiculous loaded to the brim, likely to drag ass at every shoal. But who cares? Not Johnny Walker. Not me, lighting a cigarette, ready for an adventure—for something different. The day-to-day has a way of leaving a person LOL'd to death. I *needed* this. We all did.

Still surveying my supplies, I'm the last to launch a canoe. I hesitate—and can we blame Orpheus?—but push off, jump in, and there's no turning back now. Only in the moment decision making; paddle hard on the right to miss that rock, then on the left so not to bottom out. And yes, the boat is heavy, but the drag helps against the current. And yet—steering is tricky. D.D. narrowly misses a widow-maker up ahead, back-paddling at just the right moment. And there he goes, hooting and hollering like everything was going just according to plan.

Finally the water catches up to itself and opens into a good fishing hole. Hollywood dismounts at the edge of the shoal, unraveling his throw net as I pass him gawking. And he expertly tosses the net onto a school of unsuspecting shad. My dad and D.D. are fishing up ahead, but I swing back around instead and watch the Master at work. "When's the Outdoor Channel gonna get here?" I ask. He laughs, but in three throws he's caught enough bait for the limb lines we'll set this evening.

Everything *was* going just according to plan.

We paddle on, fishing here and there, swimming from time to time to combat the heavy sunbeams of an Ozarks summer in July. We're playing tag with a bottle of homemade blackberry wine, passing it from boat to thirsty boat. The river does that—makes you thirsty. We must cover ten of the fifteen miles of our journey this afternoon if we're to get into the good catfishing tonight. And we will—gladly, the sun touching our hearts.

Five minutes pass slowly and linger, marked by a cigarette; hours pass in a blink, in a blur of several beers and miles of river twisting around rocks and trees.

At some point I fell behind, but what does it matter? As Vonnegut said, "If this isn't nice, what is?" I crack open another beer, feeling cool as a cucumber without a care in the world. I paddle along, stopping to skip rocks or jot notes. In the shade of a Sycamore tree I catch a fish, and then another. Finally it's just too easy, and I paddle along, paddle along. One sandbar reaches out into the water and forms a peninsula. I stop there for a time, set up my portable desk, and I write. Above all, the river is my muse, the place where moments of transcendental clarity are most tangible. And I write—

The sun creeps across the sky until, inevitably, moments of brilliance and boredom begin to coincide. Starting to write in circles; time to move along. It's getting late and drunk, I think to myself, laughing aloud. I load my things back into the canoe and build a rock totem at the end of the pretty peninsula. And I sit by it, munching on a granola bar, meditating on the futility of our actions and the necessity to act.

When I catch up to the others, they've banked their boats near the little dock I know belongs to Bradley Collins from the trashcan fashioned out of chicken wire and overflowing with Budweiser cans; the red ones—not Bud Light. Damn it. Just ask him.

I figure Bradley remembers me about a foot and ten years shorter. And I wonder if it's just me, but this place doesn't look anything like I remember it—aside from Bradley's little can-riddled fishing dock. I bank my boat next to the others, hop out—and it's like walking on Mars, the way I remember so distinctively this whole sandbar being just that: sand. Now it's a rocky mess, flattened out here, raised up there, probably not much for fishing. The only thing that hasn't changed is Bradley and Dad standing up there drinking beer, keeping low profiles for the rest of us. And a powerful déjà vu falls over me, standing here where I used to, if a bit less playfully now, looking up to them. Some things never change. Some things never should.

I grab a fresh beer and climb the concrete steps etched in the slope. And I add an empty Busch Light, a speck of blue, to the volcano erupting aluminum cans.

"Thought maybe you got lost. Made a wrong turn somewhere," Bradley says. And he laughs, motioning with his freehand to all the non-existent options a person has navigating a heavy canoe downriver.

"I almost *didn't* stop," I tell him. "Hardly recognized the place."

"Ain't that the truth," he says, taking a drink of his koozied Budweiser. "I mean, a place is always gonna change, but it's kinda mind blowing to see a place change this much—even in a lifetime."

"Yep," my dad says, taking a drink of beer and ruminating. "Guess it's probably gonna change again before we're done coming down here."

"Yep," Bradley says.

Yep.

Bradley laughs along with the sounds of hooting and hollering just downstream. "Sounds like they caught another one. I hope you boys are ready to clean some fish."

D.D. and Hollywood come wading back up the boats carrying full stringers of smallmouth and goggle-eye bass. Bradley wasn't kidding.

Judging by the sun we decide it's time to get going. We say our goodbyes to Bradley, add several more cans to his collection, and we depart. Only another hour or so before we reach camp; only another hour or so before the sun falls behind the trees and day makes way for night.

And we paddle along, paddle along.

Night falls. We put up camp quickly, eager to catch a catfish.

Nature speaks most clearly at night on the river. And on a night like this—the moon roughly a perfect circle, and so close; the sky shimmering and still. It's bright enough to make a flashlight unnecessary as I tie on a hook. It's eerie. It's got the owls all riled up, and so, too, my dad.

"WHO COOKS FOR YOU, WHO COOKS FOR Y'ALL?" he hoots at the top of his lungs, undeniably sounding just like a Barred owl. The resemblance is uncanny.

Immediately an owl to the north responds. And another. And one to the east, posing another question: "WHO?"

The almost existential conversation in questions imparts goosebumps.

I reach my hand into the stinking tub of raw chicken livers at my feet in the boat. The texture is something between extra chunky vomit and chilled strawberry preserves. I tear off a blob and run it through my hook twice, three times, and then once more, just to be sure. And I put a line out in the lucid dark.

My dad's still hooting at the owls in the same way that used to drive my mother—his ex-wife—crazy with embarrassment, or distaste, or whatever it was. Like so many of the senseless squabbles of the past, it doesn't matter. The world continues to turn whether we've made amends with it or not.

I finish off another bottle of wine, and about the time my cigarettes start tasting like chicken liver, I'm too drunk to care. I'm just glad we've already set the limb lines. Admittedly, I'll be even happier when we've finished checking them and planted ourselves on the riverbank to fish; or, better yet, by the fire. My balance is going. Keeping the canoe steady requires too much concentration.

I'm debating calling it a night, but—

Something nibbles at my line.

Nibble, nibble.

I freeze. Heart stops.

Nibble. Nibble, nibble.

I slowly reel in the slack, and then *jerk* the line with all the ass I can muster without falling out of the boat.

"WHO?!" I hoot.

The fish is putting up quite a fight, so I reel slowly, steadily, careful not to lose him. And I reel. And reel.

After what feels like an hour—what was very likely at least five minutes—I finally work the fish to the boat.

"Are you sure it's not a turtle?" Dad asks. And he laughs.

"It's a fish! I can tell!" I don't care what it is; I've caught something. But it's a fish.

A splashing at the surface says I've got him to the boat, but—

"Where's my net?!"

"Did you pack one?"

"Did I..." I stammer. No. No, I guess I—

SNAP!

Line broke. He's gone.

Disappointment sets in, thicker than smoke.

Bellies full, catfishing proving to be more or less a bust—Hollywood caught three or four two pounders—we sit around the campfire and dry our bones.

"Probably too much moon," my dad says. "But couldn't have asked for a better night."

And he's right.

What a night—and day. And I've looked forward to this moment, now, above all else. A good buzz, a clear mind, the combination, on occasion, staring into the fire, permits perfect solace. The river tumbles in the background, the occasional owl hoots; the world carries on. And here we are, part of it, certainly, but for a time apart, reflecting like the stars on the water. And I've found it—the temporary peace I wanted. I've been here before but still struggle to find the place when I'm looking for it. It's hid away, but I seek it out; we must seek it out.

Sparks carry in the smoke, rise and rise, turn to stars. Returning to the embers, the coals, I could stare into the fire for hours. And I intend to.

The sun's only just begun its daily climb up the blushing skyline when I emerge from my tent, head aching. The satisfaction of my having woke more or less at daylight—an accomplishment, in my mind—is slightly overshadowed by the fact that the others have already made coffee over the coals from last night's fire, packed their things, and left, fishing. I don't know how they do it. And I don't know what people did before coffee—those poor souls—but I can't help feeling spoiled, so enjoying my first cup of the day.

The morning is too beautiful not to, so I set up my desk and put my thoughts on paper. The image of a campfire is burned into my mind; something vague, wanting to be remembered—and written. But it escapes me. I should have written it down last night, whatever it was. I finish off the coffee, vaguely disappointed, as I always am, when the words aren't flowing. But if there's anything I've learned it's that inspiration comes and goes, and that, even when it's gone, it isn't gone for good. So there's no use dwelling on it.

Time returning to its normal urgency, I pack my things back into the canoe and erect another rock totem for good measure. I eat three granola bars, drink half a bottle of water in one swig, and depart.

Below Blair Bridge, I've returned to civilization. Nature holds her breath. Somewhere a dog barks. Voices, laughter, music; the world spins on. Bikini clad women sunbathe. Teenage boys throw a football around to the sound of the Red Hot Chili Peppers' spewing mad from a boom box; the boys ask "What?" a lot. Children throw rocks. An old man fishes in the water where some of the rocks go, shakes his head—at the music or the rocks, or perhaps the world in general—but keeps on fishing without so much as a bite. And I wave, paddling on.

Here, the riverbanks are lined with the skeletons of dead cars. Humanity has touched this beautiful place indifferently. And I can't help thinking of Lennie's plight in *Of Mice and Men*. That poor mouse—and poor Lennie, he never meant to hurt anything; and this poor world of ours—it was never meant to be hurt. If only intentions had more pull on causality. If only our intentions didn't fluctuate so. It would seem the human condition is but a gradual flattening of affect. And the lengths we go to, knowingly or not, in expanding this threshold say a lot about us.

I float on downriver, catching up to the others just before we reach our final destination at Patrick Bridge. I enjoy a final cigarette, musing on the releasing respite this trip has been from the reality we're returning to.

Loading everything back into the truck is always the hardest part. Back to reality; back so soon. But, worn out from two perfect days of toiling in the sun, I'm eager to return to my routine, the day-to-day I only yesterday perceived as overbearing. The truth is we need time to replenish, to reflect, to consider how lucky we are—often luckier than we give ourselves credit for. Even and perhaps especially during trying times, we must keep reminding ourselves not to take anything for granted. And then we must return to our responsibilities with patient diligence.

Leaning back in the passenger side seat adventure spent, I remember a younger version of myself who couldn't ride anywhere without falling asleep. And in as many ways as I want to believe I've grown up, there's always more growing to do when there's more living to be done.

Windows down, Waylon on the radio. I could. I could sleep.

Robert Hyers

Bosom Buddies

"ARE YOU MOTHERFUCKERS havin' a good time?" you yell into the microphone. Your crowd responds with a cascade of applause. You tilt another clear plastic cup, so thin it crushes if you grip it the wrong way, to your flame-red lips. The plastic bottled vodka burns your throat, then warms your stomach. You toss the empty cup and your over the shoulder sequin dress sparkles in the spotlight. Your silhouetted profile places its hands on its hips and stretches its neck. You bat your fake eyelashes; they come together and pull apart like Venus flytraps. A new earthquake of applause envelops you with the empty promise that this stage and the earth beneath it will crack in half and you'll die here at this moment, a star extinguished when she burned the brightest. Of course, a stranger looking in on your life might see this stage of your career as a failure. After all, after thirty years you're back in the same Jersey town you grew up in, the town next door to a superfund site whose copper stink clings to you like your designer foundation garments, the town you swore you'd never return to in that emotionally exaggerated way the female stars from your grandparent's smoky black-and-white films swore everything in. And sure, this place is tacky; the gargantuan papier mâché stiletto heel that spins high above the patrons' heads looks like a donation from the local high school's Gay-Straight Alliance's last prom. But you have been headlining this place every Friday for almost a year now. This is *your* club. And this is *your* crowd.

"You bitches ready for your another taste of Lady Agony?" you ask.

Your crowd roars louder than before.

"Then without further adieu, Lady Agony!"

You flip out a welcoming hand in Lady Agony's

direction and descend the two steps to exit stage right as Agony ascends and enters stage left. In a shadowed corner only inches from your crowd, you inspect Agony's performance of "Everything's Coming Up Roses." Agony's outfit is uninspired, a long red spaghetti-strap dress that traces her pencil-thin body juxtaposed against padded hips and big fake tits. Her wig's fire-engine red ringlets bounce as she begins lip-synching. Like her dress, her work is uninspired. But she's poised to win this season of *RuPaul's Drag Race*, and you figured you'd better get her now before she wins and her price balloons to an amount you know your club's cheap-ass owners won't pay.

    You came up with Ru. Of course, you're not as old as that fifty-three-year-old bitch; you had a fake ID in hand by the time you were twelve, the New Jersey Transit bus schedules burned into your mind with the same repetition as your times tables had been, the bus's massive roar and exhaust transporting you from a fat boy trapped in your tiny two-bedroom apartment, pillows pressed to your ears like a DJ's bulbous headphones to erase the moans of your mother and yet another stranger, to a queen in dresses that sculpted a chest normally resembling mountains of silly putty into amazing tits, a queen who controlled boys with the pout of your shiny lips and the rise and fall of your fake nails.

    You came up with Ru when Manhattan still mattered, before the island was whitewashed with million-dollar techies from the vanilla cornfields of Midwest Bumblefuck USA, when the Chelsea Piers still bubbled with banjees navigating shadows. And if the truth be told, Ru was your mother; she taught you how to refine the tricks of the trade. You loved your mother until she betrayed herself. Although Ru's true love has always been punk, she broke though with dance, with that annoying diddy "Supermodel" in '91. You swore you'd never sell out; you'd stay true to yourself, to the show tunes that had pulled you as a fresh teenager away from the mindless synthesizers of gay house music to the classics by Gershwin and Berlin and Sondheim, written back when musicians mapped their music with the same intimacy a longtime lover's fingertips can map your body's imperfections.

In your early drag days you played clubs all over the five boroughs, clusters of dance floors cramped with shadows and cut with lasers. You got dressed in the corners of coat checks, squeezed into sequins between bathroom stalls while gagging on the stench of decades-old piss tattooed on the tile walls. Eventually you got onto *Drag Race* and you thought, *This is it, I'm going to break through now.* But the judges never appreciated the Sondheim songs you had prepared, never appreciated the forties-style evening gowns you had spent all night stitching while your competition gorged on beauty sleep.

And now this Lady Agony bitch, finishing up a carbon copy of Rosalind Russell's performance as Mama Rose in the 1962 film adaptation, might actually win this season. You didn't always think Lady Agony was a bitch. Just as Ru had been your mother, you had been Agony's. She was a mess when you met her trying to look sophisticated while drinking a three-dollar cocktail at a dive bar out by Coney Island. Her rouge and eyeshadow appeared to have been applied by Miss Piggy, makeup tips Agony would later confess she had learned from her white-trash mother. From the slight bulge between her legs and the painful way her feet were squeezed into her shoes, you knew Agony had no knowledge of drag-queen essentials like how to shop for a tuck or where to find heels in men's sizes. You fixed these problems after the two of you had bonded over your parents' failures at proper attention and, more importantly, your love of show tunes. Her tastes at the time were so pedestrian; you introduced her to the better, more obscure show tunes. And now she has spent the last nineteen weeks on *Drag Race* strutting out generic Xeroxes of the smart acts and songs you worked so hard on years earlier. You feel the roar again. Lady Agony has finished.

"How'd you bitches like that one?" you ask. "You got

shit in your life? Then grow a fucking rose garden!" The applause rumbles through you and invigorates you. Someone hands you a drink. This is why you stay in this dump; these little shits love you. "We have time for one more, Agony. You up for it?"

"For this fucking crowd?" she says. Each word sounds alike, void of inflection. She sounds robotic, rehearsed. Your crowd is silent. "Of course!" she says with poorly executed enthusiasm. "But I don't think I can do it alone."

"You can't?" you say, feigning a surprise so well acted your crowd mistakes it as genuine. "Who on earth could help?"

"Get up here you stupid bitch!"

The roar of your crowd's applause returns and you feel it propel you as you ascend the stage.

"What song do you think we should do?" Agony asks. Her tone is now campy, an artifice erected to hide her lack of actual acting talent.

"How about…something from *Mame*?"

"Bosom Buddies?"

"Perfect!"

More Sondheim is released from the speakers; the muted bass line and soft percussion contrasts the screaming horns and violins of "Everything's Coming Up Roses." You lip-synch with Agony; the two of you match your mouths' movements to the throaty, smoke filled voices of Lucille Ball and Bea Arthur.

We'll always be bosom buddies

Friends, sisters, and pals

Everything goes as rehearsed. You as Bea as Vera and Agony as Lucille as Mame dance around each other during the choruses the same way Bea and Lucille did in the movie. When you tell Agony that her sense of style is almost as off as her youth, she wrinkles her face in disbelief to your audience. When Agony accuses you of being the world's biggest lush, you feign surprise with an agape mouth.

Just as Bea and Lucille did, you two are about to belt out the last chorus and march with arms locked off stage. But something comes over you. You veer from rehearsal. You tug on one of Agony's spaghetti straps. It snaps. One of her fake breasts fall out of her dress and tumbles in a blur of peach and pink to the stage floor. Agony's eyes initially widen in shock but, being the professional she thinks she is, she quickly regains her composure and pretends you did it on purpose. She reaches to rip your dress, but because you use much better material than she does, she pulls with no result. Still gripping your dress, she loses her balance and falls backwards onto the stage, pulling you with her. Sequins break free in an explosion of fractured light. You pull yourself up and pin her arms down with your knees. Sweat and liquor in the stage's felt lining soak through your pantyhose and settle on your legs. You snake your fingers through Agony's ringlets. She realizes what you're about to do and fear crawls across her face with trembling lips and a twitching eye. You pull off her wig and Agony screams to no one; the painful scream from glue pulling at skin is swallowed by Bea and Lucille's singing.

You don't know why you did it. Perhaps you thought by taking a piece of her dress, by taking the wig, you could take back some of the success she has stolen from you. Or perhaps by exposing the wig's cheap plastic netting and Agony's bald head, you thought you could expose her true ugliness. Suddenly you realize the song has ended. You pull up your knees off of Agony's arms so that she can twist her torso and face your audience. You both smile. You mime a curtsy. A trickle of awkward hand claps morph into cheers. Agony smiles; she believes they're cheering for her. But you know better.

It doesn't matter if Agony wins *Drag Race* with recycled acts that didn't even get you into the top five. It doesn't even matter if she sells out and becomes as big as Ru. You hear that familiar applause, a sound as vast and warm as the sea on those broiling hot summer days when your mother's current boyfriend would cart the three of you in his squealing broken-down stick shift to the Jersey shore. You hear that familiar applause, applause now full-bodied with a thick, throaty roar, applause you hope to someday drown in, applause Agony still believes is hers, and you know better. When the performances are over, when the eyelashes are being pulled away like caterpillars against the white light of the vanity mirror, when the wigs are seated back on their silent Styrofoam heads, you know this will always be *your* club. You know this will always be *your* crowd.

Elizabeth Hykes

Hand Blown in Ohio

They say I'm hand
blown. I don't remember.
My first memory, shivering on top of
a pump organ in a parlor. The only
heat in that room was provided by
a rarely lighted fireplace.
My close companion, a book, spoke only
when opened. At these times,
great wisdom came from his pages.
I valued his quiet companionship especially
after he tried to share his cover to warm me.

Occasionally, we played our parts in
family events. Someone would
read aloud from the book, and
I would hold a single cut rose within
me: white for weddings and baptisms,
red for anniversaries, pink for birthdays
yellow for funerals.
Distinguished by great beauty and delicacy
the roses were a thorny lot.
Not once did any acknowledge
my discomfort. Yet, it was my
calling, my duty, my privilege to be
central to life changing events.

That was long ago.
As witness to my parlor's transformation,
I experienced first, a kerosene stove, then
central heat;

family gathered in the room more
often. I started to hear voices of people
not in the room through something
called radio, and recorded music;
then tiny people in a small lighted box
called television, and now,
the internet, whatever that is.
No rose has scratched me in many a
year. My friend, the book is gone,
I know not where.

Today, they wrapped me in newspaper
and brought me here.
No longer the only one of my kind,
I am the only one labeled "hand blown in
Ohio." How I miss the pump organ, and
my old friend, the book.

Kelly Jolene

An Infection

So many times, I have loved nothing.
Too many to count, really.

Now-
Barren desert of New Mexico.
A cactus left its stinger in your palm.
I wasn't there to suck it out for you.

And this is where you went to camp
And scream about what it is you felt or believed
And here I am; never knowing any of it.

I would like to learn how to be part of your environment.
To blend in to the rocks;
to be a pebble in your backdrop.

Now-
I love too many things to count

The blue in a ring on a finger
The conspiring shape
of the mountains hunched over you
The scorpion who runs from your blanket
The shadows on the wall of a cave
The fire licking your breath
The cactus sting in your finger
The redness
The swelling

Matt Kimberlin

Masks

BILL PUT HIS FACE ON before going to the open bar. The seams were invisible to the naked eye. He left his hotel room, went downstairs. He hated people who took the elevator from the second floor. One nondescript couple embarrassed themselves on the otherwise barren dance floor. Bill didn't desire to join them, but he got a beer, wanting something in his hand. He scouted the room. A woman caught his eye. She sat alone with a few full tables close by. "Hey, you mind?" he said over the typical conference playlist.

"Yeah, sure," she said.

*

When the bar closed, they still sat together. Bill had learned her name was Amanda. He remembered from Latin classes that her name meant she who must be loved. The music died, but their conversation continued. He asked her back to his room. She agreed. They spent the night together.

The sun came up a few hours after they went to bed. Bill squinted at the open curtains. He went to shut them, but got lost in the view. The sunrise encroached on him. He felt boxed in looking at it. In the bed, Amanda yawned and smiled. She gathered her clothes, said she didn't want anything complicated. They exchanged numbers, and he said he probably wouldn't call her, which he knew was a lie.

*

Bill sat across from his boss after returning to work. His boss congratulated Bill on a new account, which tripled their expected earnings for the fiscal year. It was a short conversation, but his boss gave Bill a pat on the back before sending him out. It was an unnecessary gesture, but Bill wasn't used to recognition.

Bill strolled around the office, basking in his new celebrity. He said hello to everyone he saw under the fluorescent lights, most of whom he didn't know. Everyday social pleasantries were beyond him, but he tried. More conversations ended as a result of his small talk than began. It wasn't that he didn't care. He just couldn't engage people unless the circumstances were right. Alcohol helped.

*

Bill removed his face when he got home. The skin peeled away, leaving his musculature visible. Red flesh interlocked with tendons in a macabre postmodern mural. His cheekbones pursed against the tissue, forming bubble-like pockets, and the white of his eyes and teeth was magnified by the skinless flesh. The outline of where his skin began and ended was well-defined, a floppy pseudo-circle that hung like dog ears. He looked like a character from kabuki theatre, meant to scare children into believing in some divine enterprise.

He wondered if faces were necessary things. Everything worked well enough without them. He always lived alone, kept the curtains drawn, but he breathed, ate, spoke, did all normal functions. He wouldn't have met Amanda without his face. He considered calling her, but thought against it. He reminded himself that he should focus on Gabby.

Gabby was his new client and latest fling, a business woman from the suburbs, probably cheating on her husband. Her finger was losing its tan, maybe a recent divorce. She was the kind of woman he'd always wanted to have an affair with– older, but not too much older.

Bill set his face on the nightstand in a pan of murky liquid to keep it hydrated. He flipped on the television, tried not to mar his evening with thoughts of change. He liked how things were going. He gave it about three months before his life exploded back on him, but it was worth it in the meantime.

He let his muscles relax. They were tense when covered. He wondered if the rest of his muscles were that tense. He considered trying to remove all of his skin, but thought it might be uncomfortable, especially with clothes. Instead, he let the air flow over him, a moving, comforting blanket.

*

While Bill was writing a report the next day, three people came by his desk. Each offered congratulations on his success. He escaped to the water cooler.

"Hey, Bill?"

He turned around. A woman he had never seen before in his life knew his name. He tried to hide his discomfort.

"Oh, I'm Amy," she said. "Wouldn't expect you to know that. I'm new here. I heard you're the go-to around here. Can I pick your brain on a few things?"

Bill nodded, and they talked for several minutes. Amy was straightforward and had a genuine smile. Bill answered all the questions he could and directed her to the boss for the rest.

He stayed at the water cooler a while. Several people walked by. Advising Amy solidified his new office role. Looks of admiration—and even jealousy—drifted his way with growing frequency. His star was rising.

*

"It's been great," Gabby said.

"I'm glad you came into the fold," Bill said. He felt constrained by his face in the evening but recognized its necessity. "The boss is glad to have your business."

"I think you're the one who's really happy," she said.

"Not complaining," he said. "That's for sure."

They sat together at one of the nicest restaurants in town. Bill had never been there, and he was glad Gabby had asked him. That was her only rule; the inviter gets the tab. It was their third date, and he thought she was probably tired of Chinese. He knew she was fond of wine.

"How do you do it?" she asked.

"What?"

"Never mind."

The question hung in his mind for the rest of the night, even as Gabby paid the tab.

*

The boss called Bill into the office later that week. Since Bill hadn't accomplished anything new, he sat outside the office like a kid in school wondering which rule he had broken. He wasn't used to reprimands.

Bill stepped in and took a seat, his hands fumbling on his knees. The boss moved a paperclip sculpture out of the way. Bill stared at the sculpture, unable to figure out what it was at first. He decided that it had to be a dolphin when his boss spoke up. "You know you didn't file the trip with corporate?"

"No, sir," Bill said.

"It's going to take a couple of weeks to re-file the paperwork. I don't have to tell you what that means."

"Man hours?"

"You're a smart one. Not a big deal this time, but don't make it a habit. Understood?"

"I apologize, sir. It won't happen again."

"Good, I don't like repeating myself."

Bill left. He didn't have anything else to say. He felt like people were looking at him, but they didn't have admiration in their eyes anymore. It was like they were waiting for something.

*

Bill had a date with Amanda that evening, so he didn't take off his face. They had a pleasant meal, decent service, and a nice bottle of wine. Everything went well until Amanda coughed. Bill asked what was wrong. She pointed to his lips. He felt them. The right side was drooping. He excused himself to the restroom.

Looking in the restroom mirror, he pushed the flesh back into place as gently as possible. His face had never done that. It looked like something heavy was hanging from his lips, but the flesh stayed in place once he pushed it back into place.

*

Bill contemplated not taking his face off to sleep. Maybe he removed it too much, or it might have been losing form. How would people react to him without his face? Would they be intrigued by the sight? Would they be frightened? Maybe it was a worthwhile experiment to go somewhere without his face.

He couldn't remember anyone seeing him without his face. He learned how to take it off in college when he had no roommates. He'd never had a serious enough relationship to worry about a significant other. No one else had a key to his apartment. He didn't like the idea of giving a key to anyone. If and when a relationship took a turn for the worst, he didn't want to come home to his apartment ablaze due to repressed anger management issues.

Bill decided it was best to keep his face on. He had trouble getting to sleep, and the fan didn't feel as nice.

*

In the morning, both sides of Bill's lips hung below his chin, and his nose looked like an icicle, ready to drip. He pushed the surrealist pieces back into place, reconstructing the found art of his face. The image in the mirror didn't feel like his face anymore.

*

Bill bought a mirror to keep at his desk on his way to work. He made minor adjustments throughout the day, but the skin kept falling faster. By the afternoon, he had to look in the mirror every five minutes to ensure his face remained in proper working order. In the morning it had been his lips, but by then his eyebrows and cheeks were flopping down. The boss called him in at three.

"Have a seat," the boss said, pushing aside the paperclip sculpture. "Do you have any medical issues, Bill?"

"No, sir."

"Are you aware that your face is falling off?"

Bill hesitated. "No, sir."

"Well, it is. I can't do anything about an unseemly medical condition, but I would appreciate if you'd take the rest of the day off if this is an outbreak of some sort. Don't worry. It won't come out of your sick days. Take tomorrow if you need it and get well soon."

Bill hesitated for a second. He wanted to fight the decision, to put his life on his own terms, but he thought better of it. It wouldn't have accomplished anything, and the time alone could have done some good, so he gave in. "Yes, sir."

Bill went to his desk, picked up his briefcase, but he noticed a splotch of skin on it. His face was melting like candle wax. He ran to the restroom, trying to catch as much of the ooze as possible. A trail of wax-like skin stuck to the ground in his wake.

He stared at the putty in his hands. Pushing it back on, he constructed little more than half a face. It was enough to get him out of the building, but the dripping didn't stop.

A janitor was scraping Bill's face off of the ground as Bill walked out of the lobby. Bill's coworkers said goodbye with big smiles.

"Are you leaving for the day? See you tomorrow."

"Take as much time as they give you; I'd try to get Monday off, too. No one likes to come in on a Monday."

"Have a good evening. Try to get some rest. You look like you need it."

Bill's face was gone by the time he got to his car, and he couldn't go back to get it.

*

Gabby didn't want to cancel their date. She didn't believe he was ill and insisted on coming over to see him if he was. She said it was the mother in her. He didn't think it would go well, but he wasn't sure what to do. If he said no, she might have thought he was hiding someone else in his life. There were no good options.

Bill answered the door without his face. Gabby rambled on about homeopathic remedies for every ailment until she saw his blood red no-face face. "You weren't kidding about not feeling well."

"Yeah," Bill said. "I wasn't."

"I'm going to walk away now," Gabby said. "I hope you won't take it personally if you never hear from me again. It's just that your face is gone. That's disturbing."

"Of course," he said, shutting the door before she walked away. Personal relationships were the least of his concerns if he couldn't get a new face. He took a long bath, letting the steam relax his muscles before he lay down to bed.

*

When Bill woke up, all of the skin and hair on his head had pooled into a hardened mass on his pillow. He had trouble raising his head at first. The malleable substance stuck to the back of his head until it snapped like a rubber band.

Bill stared at the solid puddle on his pillow. He had never been a thinker. He followed instructions for the most part. He had nothing but time to think now, and he wondered if his condition was permanent. Could there be some sort of skin graft? Would he look normal in a year or two if his cells were replicated in a Petri dish?

He thought about whether they still had freak shows. Maybe he could have found a new career. He imagined himself on stage next to the bearded lady and the amazing lizard boy, finding true love with the most tattooed woman in the world. People could have stared at him without any shame. They wouldn't have to keep the smile on or be polite. Their revulsion could have been on clear display, uninhibited by tact and decency. He would've been the star of the show, the man with no skin, completely exposed to the world with nothing to protect him from its gaze.

A call from the office broke his concentration. Bill didn't pay much attention to the rant, but he was fired. He had to pick up his things, skin disease or not. Bill decided to go get his stuff and get it over with.

*

Skin dripped off Bill's fingers as he opened the door to the lobby, and his shoes overflowed with goo. No one batted an eye. His new former colleagues expressed sympathies. The Stepford coworkers made no attempt to ask him about his condition, but the janitor scoffed when he saw Bill leaving another mess.

Layers of skin fell from Bill's hands, and it hurt him to pick things up. He gathered everything into a single box, leaving the office computer, but stealing office supplies. Several paperclips fell and got stuck in the goo trail he left behind. He didn't feel the need to make more of a scene. No one could have forgotten him, even if they wouldn't ever admit it.

*

Bill noticed a missed call from Amanda. Apprehensive, he called her back as he drove home. The exposed muscles in his hands hurt whenever anything touched them. Even sitting was starting to get painful.

"I heard you got fired," Amanda said. "Want to talk about it when I get off work?"

Bill thought about saying no, but he wanted company.

*

Amanda knocked on the door at ten after six. She hadn't even gone home to change out of her work clothes.

Bill answered the door. He waited for her to back away, but she didn't.

"Your skin is gone," Amanda said.

"Yeah," Bill said. "I know."

"That's really strange."

"I've heard that."

"Can I come in?"

First appeared in *Curbside Splendor*

Mary Knobbe

Michaella

WE MET OUR JUNIOR YEAR of college and became instant friends. With her wide grin, boisterous laugh, and kind heart, she was the kind of the girl everyone on campus noticed. She was a mover and a shaker. I was a little nervous. We lived in the same dorm – she as an R.A. and I as the front desk manager. Our senior year, we were inseparable. We ran with the same friends, went to the same concerts, and drank the same beers. After college, she began her life of adventure. She taught in Appalachia and wrote stories in Tucson. She took bus trips and met strangers. I went to work. I started a family. The things you were supposed to do. I had a plan – a nine-to-five job near my family and a red-brick house, my own version of the white-picket fence. Our lives, once totally in sync, became separate roads that seemed to wind farther and farther apart. I heard from her sporadically, and she heard from me less.

Years later, she showed up in my hometown. She'd found a lover and thought it might be forever. She saw the old me hidden under my thick layers of responsibility and adulthood. A lurking ghost of the carefree, creative 20-year-old I used to be. We met for coffee, and we decided to write. The first year or two, it was haphazard and half-hearted on my part. I had papers to grade and bottoms to diaper, but she didn't give up. Our meetings became more regular, my writing more earnest. I had pages of stories where I rediscovered my own adventure of young, requited love, motherhood, and rock 'n roll. One day in early February, she met me at our regular coffee house/writing lab with excitement in her eyes. She found a retreat. A perfect road trip for two gals ready to shuck the obligations of regular life because, now, she too had papers to grade and a husband to care for. I smiled and said, *Maybe*.

Months later, we found ourselves bunked by a river in the middle of the budding Ozark Mountains. For the first time, I took the dream of my eight-year-old self seriously. I wrote and wrote and wrote. That day, with a dose of liquid courage, I shared my secret dream with strangers. Now, still high on the acceptance from our fellow artists, we were not-so-quietly tip-toeing our way in the dark down to the river, intent on living our lives to the fullest. As the crisp April air chilled what little skin I left bare, I gave myself a pep talk. This is what writers did, I told myself. They threw caution to the wind and lived a wild life. They went skinny dipping in April in a river rushing through the mountains. After our five-minute walk to the shore, we stripped down. It was too cold, I said, stopping when I got down to a bikini of a bra and sensible underwear and only dipping my toes into the frigid water. She started singing a song with words I didn't know, her voice strong and true. Joy bubbled up from my depths, and I laughed at the return of my own voice. My skin tingled as I submerged myself, baptism by ice, a new sense of purpose crystalizing.

TIMOTHY LEYRSON

The Genesis

He never felt oppression in Compton's summer heat.
In 1989 he could barely speak.

Not six years old, shy and nervous,
but he could tell the news was showing disservice.

He wasn't raised in the country.
He had a backyard and saw police;

With the Nancy Reagan in tow from the White House
LAPD used a tank to break open a "crack house."
Tenants were arrested for sleeping while black
as police searched in vain for any signs of smack.

Thirsty for knowledge, he
never doubted college,

but dissecting frogs was
boring, there was no allegory.

Math formulas were repetitive;
in gym, why be competitive?

To score a point or win the race
just knock the glasses off his face
to leave him blind
as Doctor Frankenstein's
sense of morality.

Unknowingly

        tainted by the color of skin,
he was cornered in bathrooms by taunts thick with sin.

White pride was injured
because his brain set the curve.

He learned to keep the fight tight, don't give up space,
they can't call you *nigger* when they're blue in the face.

By the way, fuck them, he's not "just-so-well-
spoken," while they saw him as a token

his pen scorches paper with fiery rhymes.
Ever since Longfellow told him of Paul Revere's ride
exposing the secret of how to travel through time.

The horse hoof beat
along cobblestone street,

a man raced through blackest night.
He spread the warning,
"The British are coming."

"So take up your guns & fight." *Huey said.
2 shots in the dark now Huey's dead.*[1]

[1] *Lyrics taken from "Changes" by Tupac Shakur*

ANDREW MARSHALL

Black Crickets

Black crickets are black dreams
that scratch against the inside of cardboard boxes,
crawling across the bathroom tile,
leaping into pockets
and cereal boxes.
Cracking underneath my feet,
in the garage
because I don't watch where I step.
They drift dead into the corners,
until bits of antenna and wing and leg
become tangled in dog hair, dust,
dead pills bugs, and wire casing—
red like an intestine yanked.
But,
if I lift that stripped wire,
blow it clean
in my clean hand,
free of dust
and cricket bits,
my eyes closed
my body warm,
tight in blankets,
lucky in sleep
the casing can be dry,
flexible, remade
into a heart,
a ring,
a line
to follow
anywhere.

John Monagle

Sitting on the Ledge

A solid heaviness is in my chest
as storm clouds gather above the mountains
across the valley. I hear footsteps
of someone approaching. I turn
and see a dark skinned, dark
haired short, muscular man stand
beside me. He asks if there is anything
he can do for me. I pull a football sized
rock from within my chest
and give it to him. I ask if he can
take it to the ridge above us
and drop it. He nods.

As he hikes to the ridge,
I sit down and savor the
lightness of myself.
Storm clouds quickly float away,
revealing the mid-morning sun.

I hear him saying "Man, this rock
is getting bigger and heavier."
A few seconds later, I hear it drop.
A rock slide begins with several small boulders.
I watch the rocks slide over the cliff,
then look up to see him standing nearby.
I smile as he shrugs his shoulders.
He turns around and leaves.

ANNIE NEWCOMER

An Emotional Response to C.K. William's "Near the Haunted Castle" In a Workshop at River Pretty

Poets fight gangs: Young girl saved by Policeman's empathetic words.

OK. Let's go back to find where the truth is...Back to the beginning. In the beginning was love, right? No, in the beginning ... the bullet...

A regular "William Tell World" - minus the arrows. Instead we have guns. William carefully cocks his gun, and blows the apple to smithereens right off of Adam's head. Next, Eve steps up. W.T. places his second apple, this time on her head, and Eve starts to shiver like she's really scared. Like she's seen this all before. Like she has a premonition that WT isn't paying as close attention. Like if Tell should miss the apple and hit her heart nobody's even going to care... it won't really matter... She's just a girl... there's lots of other Eves out there to replace her. And so it will go on and on forever more.

"This is a story. You don't have to think about it. It's make believe." It's like the truth but not really the truth because who really cares about the truth these days? Who wants to spoil a really good argument, a good poem or, for that matter, a nicely polished red apple, with the truth? I'm just saying. So let's not even bother going way back to the beginning. Let's just go back to say, today, like this morning, to a street in Chicago or inner city Kansas City or the Poetry Festival at Bacha Khan University in Charsadda, Pakistan. Is that OK?

Now I don't have a lot of time. Especially not for a story, especially this story with girls running around in it, so let's sum this all up- we've got a princess- related to the same princesses who've been lugging those peas around for centuries. And the same gang, some people never change no matter what story you place them in. Don't ask me why. It's just the way it is. And while I'm at it, I'm going to put you all in the story too- yeah you, might as well make you all working writers. So here you are in the story and each of you gets a vote - some even two, so let's all decide together what changes to make. Real quick- let's ask the poet if he really wants to switch places with the "Man in Blue" - you know , the one with the holsters , the one who kisses his family each morning real tenderly because he might not see his children again that night. And, yeah, that means this policeman, well he gets the pen, you know the pen lying on the table, you remember the table, if you didn't sleep in and miss workshop that is, the table that can actually think, the thoughtful table? Yeah, that's the one. Up next, the princess. What to give her? Maybe respect, the same wages as men. Heck, maybe we'll even vote her in as the next president of the United States. That leaves the gangs. I know. Let's give each gang member a pea. Yes, let's give them each a freakin' pea.

But this story has gone off the tracks, and you know, I didn't pack my sweater and suddenly it's gotten chilly here in *River Pretty* - yes, all of a sudden we're feeling the crisp autumn morning and I'm having a brain freeze. But, what the heck? What do I know? Call myself a poet. That's a joke. Heck, I can hardly even keep track of my pen.

BILL OAKLEY

Losing Things I Love Through Inattention

Taking a pan of kitchen waste to the compost pile
I stopped to talk to the remains
of the Chinese elm
A tree I loved
Loved for it's shape Loved
for it's origin Loved for it's
sprit and soul
DEAD
because I was DISTRACTED
Dead from simple-extended lack of attention

While caressing a dead branch and telling Elm
I love her
I realized this tree is not just a
metaphor but an example
of a pattern in my life

If during times of no rain
I can't find the awareness to turn on the fucking hose
how compassionate am I ?

Distractions come and go
Love comes and stays
Lives on if acknowledged and nurtured

drifts away if untended

Little Tiny Hand Jobs

What kind of hand job do you prefer
myself I LOVE little tiny hand jobs
don't get me wrong I am not talking about hand jobs performed
by little tiny underaged hands
NO
i mean hand jobs that last only an instant
short and oh so sweet
as it was with that guy who I picked up on the dance floor
who kissed eyes wide open
just as I do
eyes searching for and finding JUST WHAT I needed
his hand doing all the right things
no holding back an instant
EXPLOSION of joy

or that woman who picked me up on the dance floor
her mouth so perfectly formed
her words alone almost made me cum
so that when she touched my cock
I came and came until my prostate was empty
and my ears rang with the echo of her voice

these are the little tiny hand jobs that still haunt my dreams

What kind of hand job do you prefer?

TODD OSBORNE

Counting Rings

trees offer their age in rings
rock dropped in still water
       and sifting deeper

you can read the tree like a history
of frosts in a forgotten language
       take this one
taller than the house I grew up in

still reaching while I remain stunted unable to attain
       tantalus and figs
anything higher than my outstretched arm
anything purer than the rootless ground I tread

yes; trees give us age in their rings and we?
our bones cut me open
       expose cartilage and marrow

count my years in scar tissue
know that in hard years trees
       contract and we expand

the sound of forest rustling then silence
       expectant limbs brushing

and morning light breaking through
       warming in their grasp

J.T. Robertson

While Skimming Requests for Proposals

After Jennifer Murvin's "While Reading My Students' Stories"

ELIGIBLE APPLICANT MUST be a registered 501(c)3 nonprofit, tribal government, local government, state entity. For-profits and individuals are ineligible. Proposals must show requested funds will make a significant impact on the community, on lives, on those in need, on the hard-to-serve, disadvantaged, homeless, at-risk, underserved, undereducated, unemployed, underemployed. Involved. Impactful. Efficient. Effective.

List anticipated outcomes. List measurable results. List names and qualifications of responsible staff. List each board member's age, ethnicity, employer, email, phone, fax, connections, position, tax bracket, giving. List total number of volunteers. List lobbying activities. List compensation and benefits of executive staff. List income sources over $10,000 received past 6, 12, 24 months. List square footage and occupancy. List rental income. List capital purchases. List staff amenities, if applicable. List sub-contractors. List suppliers.

One-inch margins, Times New Roman, Arial, 10-point, 12-point, black only, full color, electronic signatures, live signatures in blue ink, one-inch three-ring binders. Logic models complete using approved template. No blank boxes. Detailed descriptions of each program component in one-inch boxes. Submit a signed IRS form 990 filed in the past 15 months. Provide a state certificate of good standing signed within the last 90 days. Provide a current balance sheet. Provide an updated audit. Provide eight collated copies plus original with live signatures and dates. Submissions must arrive in a sealed envelope. Only emailed submissions accepted.

Clients must be between the ages of 16 to 21, 18 to 35, 30 to 65, 60 and older. Client income must fall below 30% of area median income, above 30% area median income. Clients must be from neighborhoods with poverty rates 10% above national, regional, state average. Clients must be disabled. Clients must prove veteran status and honorable discharge. Homeless clients must meet the published definition in appendix II.2.B. Clients must provide family income information, social security card, birth certificate, test scores, drug tests, assurances, approvals, signatures. Clients must not be discriminated against based on age, race, sexuality, gender, ability, disability, origin, medical history, sex-offender or ex-offender status.

Clients cannot be required to attend religious services to receive services. Program curriculum must be completed within 30 days, 60 days, 90 days of entry. Client status on entry and exit outcomes must be documented. Documentation may include any or all of the following: case manager notes, intake forms, exit forms, surveys, scribbles, paystubs, timesheets, certificates, diplomas, word-of mouth, sworn affidavits, notarized forms. Client data must be tracked using our secure database. Data must be entered within three business days. Data must be kept confidential to respect client privacy. Contact must be maintained with clients for a minimum 90 days on exit. On-going supportive services and case management must be provided for a minimum 12 months after successful completion.

On-going supportive services and case management are ineligible costs under interim rule 435.7.25. Service costs should not be included in the supportive services budget. Operations costs should not be included in the operations budget. Required budget and budget narrative templates are available for download on our website. Capital and unrestricted line items are ineligible. Salaries should be included only for direct service staff. Administration cost cannot exceed 7%, 8%, 10%. Funding requires 50%, 75%, 100% match from non-government sources. Invoices for reimbursement due last day of quarter during grant period. Applicants must provide a detailed plan for future funding after foundation funding ends. Cost-sharing and in-kind services through collaboration encouraged.

Collaboration is key to a competitive proposal. Required coalition must include representatives from the Department of Social Services, Department of Human Services, Department of Housing and Urban Development, Department of, Office of, Department of. Key stakeholders include local housing authority, local government, area service providers, community groups, Workforce Investment Board, citizen groups, neighborhood associations, client's families, volunteers, board members, individual donors, friends, neighbors, others.

Questions must be submitted by June 21st, in writing, by email, in person. Questions will not be accepted after April 14th. Inquiries by phone will remain unanswered. Applications must be turned in before the deadline. Submissions must be postmarked by November 13th. Applicants are encouraged to submit before 4:59 pm on February 15th. Applications will be reviewed and ranked in the order they arrive. The foundation board will meet, the commission will meet, the program staff will meet and forward their recommendations. Final decisions will be made at the monthly, quarterly, annual meeting.

Applicants may only submit one application in response to this solicitation. This request for proposals does not constitute approval or guarantee of funding.

Allen Ross

Sun Chips

He hid the light where
no one would look,
a bag of Sun Chips.
Granted, it made a lot of noise,
but who listens for light?
He was proud of his ability
to hide such brilliance, and
conceal his elation with a
sad dark attitude.
Most life forms grow weak and pale,
then soon die out when light fails.
But a light hearted disguise
can withstand extreme exposure.

A Lifetime of Memories with the Sticky Food Group

-after Michael Burns

With no knowledge of poetic forms I listened as
Marcus read a prop for the class about pancakes
and my thoughts oozed, but not sweet like maple syrup.

*

As autumn as a sorghum mill, my family's annual drive
through the Ozarks would not be complete without a
jar of that cheap imitation of maple syrup.

*

I bought a house on Grand Avenue in Carthage,
the main route of the Maple Leaf Festival Parade,
causing me to question if we were pouring it on too thick.

*

Although, it's not Super Glue, maple syrup can adhere
household utensils for years if allowed to dry correctly.

*

As a child growing up in rural Missouri, I had resentment
towards my grandparents for putting Cairo syrup on
pancakes and then apologizing for not having sorghum.

*

My brother, who considers himself a Rock Music authority,
claims the Rolling Stones wrote the song, "Sticky Fingers"
after a food fight started during a breakfast break.

*

When I was ten my parents took me to an International House
of Pancakes where I learned there are other syrups,
besides maple, that are very delicious.

*

I lament it was not possible to pour maple syrup all over Michael
so he could have stuck around longer to make more pancakes.

SOPHFRONIA SCOTT

The Payoff Letter

Chase Home Finance
3415 Vision Drive
Columbus OH 43219
800-689-9136 Customer Care
800-689-0542 TDD/ Text Telephone

April 1, 2012

Sophfronia Scott
62 Turkey Hill Road
Newtown, CT 06470

Re: Home Mortgage Loan # ******2542: **Payoff Letter**

Dear Sophfronia Scott:

THIS LETTER IS TO ACKNOWLEDGE that Chase Home Finance (Chase) has received the funds to pay off your mortgage loan referenced above. Chase will forward an original executed release of lien for recording to the recorder's office in the county where the property is located.

    Until the release is processed, this letter will serve as proof that Chase has received the payoff funds. Within 30 days from receiving the payoff funds, Chase will forward any funds we receive in excess of the payoff amount and any remaining escrow funds for you. Unless notified of an address change, Chase will send the overpayment or escrow refund you are entitled to as a result of this payoff and your 1098 year-end interest statement to the mailing address used for sending this letter. To prevent a delay, please inform us of any change in your mailing address, but since your goal has been to always remain in this home such a change is highly unlikely.

You may contact the county or town recorder's office for information about the time to process the lien release and how to obtain a recorded copy.

If Chase collected escrow funds for paying your mortgage taxes or insurance, you are now responsible for the payment of these items. Please contact your homeowner's insurance agent and your taxing authority to advise them of the address to forward future bills and correspondence. As long as these payments are kept current—they are usually made on a yearly basis—you will not have to fear losing your home as was your concern each month when your mortgage payment came due.

You may now tell your son you have increased the probability that he can remain in the home for his entire childhood, and he will most likely have a tidy inheritance coming his way, depending on the health of the real estate market, when he is grown and you and your spouse are deceased. He may continue to tack up with pushpins, and not wall putty, the posters and drawings he makes for his room. The holes in the drywall do not seem to bother you as it does other parents and, after all, the walls are now yours. When he is a teenager, he may want to paint his room something other than the sunny yellow you thought appropriate when he was a baby. A gentle reminder for him to apply a bit of spackle to the tiny perforations before he does so should be adequate. The color black should be discouraged as rigorously as possible.

You are likely also thinking of the pencil markings in the basement mudroom, indicating the increase in your son's height from the age of two. No one will paint over them now, at least not for many more years, unless you choose to do so yourself.

It is recommended, however, that a thorough decluttering take place at least once a year, focusing on the attic and basement spaces. This will prevent the property from developing hoarding issues and keep your home comfortable for years to come. Clutter accumulates in a more determined fashion when a family raises a child from infancy in one house. The four plastic storage bins of clothing, labeled with masking tape "0-3 months" and "6-9 months," for example, are no longer necessary. If you were going to pass them on to a friend or family member you would have done so by now. Goodwill (www.Goodwill.org) or Big Brothers Big Sisters (www.bbbs.org) will arrange a home pick up for your convenience.

If you cannot bear to discard any of your son's belongings after he has grown up and left the home, we suggest you ship them to his house to dispose of as he chooses.

But perhaps it is wrong to focus on this when all you really care about is the new certainty that you will always have your office, the red room with the yellow chaise and the connected library with the wall of books and your writing table. All this time you feared losing it when all you really had to do was let go of it and write.

This is the space that matters to you most. The large window with the plastic white lines that make it look like separate panes of glass frames the sun rising over the hill in the woods in the morning to shine on your desk just so. It is fitting to have such big windows, especially in autumn when the yellow leaves just outside blaze and fire your creativity. But then all windows are important to you. You moved into this house in January 2005, with a six-month old infant and only one car. Your one requirement was that the home be light and airy enough that no matter how long you spent in it each day with your baby you would never feel confined. The house turned out to be so bright, in fact, that you can follow the sun all around the property if you like, but these days you can stay in your office. This is the room where you sit on red cushions in a corner to pray like Thomas

Merton, and you nap on the chaise like George Sands, and at your desk you write your letters like Anais Nin. It is yours now for as long as you like.

Your spouse, likewise, can keep the odd, sapphire blue color in his basement recording studio although, if forced to sell, you were more concerned with having to take down the extra walls and soundproofing he installed to create his perfect haven. You will still hear the sounds of hesitant trombonists beneath your feet as he teaches private lessons. You will also, unfortunately, have that eerie sense of a voice coming through the walls until you remember it's most likely his muffled singing as he rehearses for his next gig. Please try to keep in mind your home is not haunted nor is there any record of it ever having been so.

Since you know you will stay in this house now you must be more vigilant in regularly cutting back the row of dwarf lilac bushes in front of the house. Otherwise they will become overgrown and you will have to admit neglect and defeat and have the bushes removed. You did not pay off your mortgage to experience such heartbreak.

Chase's goal is to provide the highest level of quality service to each of our customers. If you have any questions, please contact Customer Care at 800-689-9136.

We appreciate the opportunity to have serviced your mortgage loan and hope that you will contact Chase for your future financial needs.

Sincerely,

Reconveyance Department, Chase Home Finance

Reconveyance Services for Alaska, Nevada and California are provided by J.P. Morgan Chase Custody Services, Inc.

Heather Sharfeddin

Gift Giving in America: A Guide

LORETTA OCCASIONALLY STANDS over the bathroom sink with a pair of sharp scissors and whacks away at her own locks because she's left them too long and they are suddenly and urgently driving her mad. She has the softest red-brown curls that can frizz up like a freak show attraction if she neglects them. Which she does. I knew that she could sometimes look like a Wensleydale sheep when I married her, but it's her focus—her tendency to leave off with the less important things when she's working—that I find charming.

Loretta and I are freelance writers. Giving up your corporate marketing job to become a full-time writer sounds glamorous, but it's really one of scrambling to get short-term gigs that you can do mostly from home and that will pay enough to get you through the month. I don't mean get you through in style—I mean just the basics like food, rent, gas. These jobs come along with all the frequency of a 100 year flood, so you have plenty of time to work on your own stuff in between. Unless you accidentally tap into a corporate vein of unmet need, then look out; you're working like a fool again writing technical manuals, or editing English translations, or developing curriculum and sooner or later you'll have to tell them to get their own goddamn writer. Otherwise you may as well still have your old day job.

Loretta and I live in a musty one-bedroom rental house in Neskowin, Oregon. It's just far enough outside Portland that no one really expects us to drive the two hours each way for evening literary events, but close enough that if one of us won a major award, we could handle the publicity aspect of it in a major metropolitan area that has a reputation for good literature. She's a poet, and I'm working on a memoir about the death of my brother when we were still boys. The real reason we live here is because we both dreamed of living at the beach and nothing says you're committed to your dream like actually doing it.

Loretta's been ghost writing a book on how to be successful in business for a local retired guy whose company employs a large percentage of our rural county, and she's been hard to live with lately. The man is a jerk; she knew it going in. I warned her when she took the job that she'd regret it. "You'll either hate him or hate the book by the end of this." He may have built the biggest fish processing plant in the region, but years of near hysterical praise from his workers, the school officials where he donated a soccer field, and the local business community have, in his later years, given him a god complex.

And he's not shy about offering advice. Loretta assured me she could handle his ego, but last night when she was reading through his comments on the four-hundred-plus loose pages, double-spaced with one-inch margins, she hurled the entire manuscript against the bedroom wall, shouting, "This asshole can go fuck himself if he thinks he can tell me how to structure a sentence."

After I made her a cup of cocoa with two shots of whiskey, we pieced the manuscript back together, one page at a time. Her tantrums kind of turn me on.

Though our house is old and a bit run-down, it overlooks the Pacific Ocean and one of the biggest monoliths on the coast. When the tide is low we can walk most of the way around it. The house is tubular and constructed from bent aluminum siding, like a wide, slightly flattened culvert that juts from land out over a bluff. The deck is supported on stilts that are anchored to the rocks above our windswept coastline. The house was built in 1974 and it still has its avocado green appliances. We pulled out the shag carpet, which was growing tiny mushrooms near the sliding door, and replaced it with bamboo. Loretta painted the interior cyan blue, so even on the stormiest days, which are most days from November to July, it's bright and cheerful. Regardless of its age and condition, its location is prime and it would rent for more than eight-hundred a week if it were in the rental pool. It's on a dead end street of similar houses that see a steady turn-over of vacationers and part-time dwellers. Aside from the elderly couple three doors down, we're the only ones who live here year-round, and the owners of the other houses have gotten to know us in an attempt to spy on their own properties through our eyes.

My uncle Sean owns this house, and he rents it to Loretta and me for nine-hundred a month. In exchange, we do all the upkeep. Uncle Sean has let us live here on the cheap for six years now, and he hasn't made any noise about ending the agreement. Loretta and I wonder how we would make it if we had to move back to Portland. One of us, maybe both, would have to take a day job again. Though Uncle Sean calls this his "contribution to art," it's a two-way street. And he called me a couple of weeks ago about a job. A friend of his consults with foreign companies interested in breaking into the American market. He had a team of writers and translators already hard at work, but there was one rogue project that he needed to outsource. Uncle Sean recommended me because I have an MFA in writing, which apparently means more to international clients than awards or publication credentials.

"It's easy," he had said over the phone. "A primer on gift giving customs in America."

"Gift giving customs?" I asked. It wasn't a topic I'd thought much about.

"Yeah, something like that," he said, and I heard his assistant telling him he was late for an appointment. "It'll pay well. These international business people really like smarty pants like you."

"I don't know anything about gift giving."

"Make it up," he said.

Who was I to say no? The man rarely asks for anything in exchange for the great deal he gives us on the house.

"Sure. Give me the contact info."

When I got off the phone I told Loretta, who was making toast.

"Gift giving?" She grunted, her hair wild. She was dressed in sweatpants and a long-sleeved tee shirt. She wore wool socks and Birkenstocks, just like people imagine when they think of Oregon. But in our defense, it's damp here.

I got started that afternoon because I didn't have much paying work at the time. *Gift giving in America. Section 1. Holidays.* I stared at the crisp words on my screen. Starting a project is always the hardest and the most invigorating. But then again, this wasn't a choice assignment. I thought about the holidays that my protestant family celebrated: Thanksgiving, Christmas, Easter, Memorial Day, Independence Day, and Labor Day. Did they want a pop-culture type write-up on gift giving, or something that delved into different religious groups? I talked to the Li Ma, the assigned client contact, on the phone, and after a few minutes I was able to discern from her broken English that the pamphlet was for visiting business people and their spouses. They wanted to make a good impression, and after they themselves had received tins of caramel corn, chocolates, and cookies with brightly colored cards from their American partners last holiday season, they were unsure whether it was appropriate to send gifts from China, such as jasmine tea, at holidays. They thought something more American would be a good idea. And they didn't want to be surprised during their visits by holidays and occasions where exchanging gifts was expected.

I had the sense that I was creating new international customs from scratch in my little house overlooking the Pacific. Rain pelted the patio doors in heavy gusting buckets, and

Loretta got up from her desk and placed rolled towels along the bottom to keep the cold out. We'd sealed it with silicone recently, but a bitter wind could still find its way in. She turned on the lamps as she returned to her desk, despite it being ten o'clock in the morning.

I need coffee when I'm working on a challenging project, but I'd accidentally broken the coffee press when I was washing dishes a week or so back. Neskowin doesn't have anything like a Target store, so replacing it meant a trip down the coast to Lincoln City. Like I said, I didn't have a lot of paying work at the moment, so I made due with some black tea, though it wasn't the same.

Christmas, I thought, sipping my over steeped Earl Grey. I tipped back in the ergonomically correct leather chair that Loretta had found for me at Saint Vincent de Paul and conjured my fondest Christmas memories. As a kid we visited my grandmother in Montpelier, Vermont every other year. It was a long trip—three or four flights, plus a one-hour drive over snow and ice in a rented car. It typically took us a full day from Oregon, though it was not uncommon to get stuck in Denver or Chicago or Newark and end up spending the night. The getting there sucked, but once we were in Vermont it was Gramma and sugar cookies, candy canes, and a real spruce tree. This was before my brother died, and we would lie awake in our beds, listening through the thin walls of that Victorian house as the adults filled the stockings and placed the gifts under the tree. I don't know when we stopped believing in Santa, or if we ever did. That didn't matter. What mattered was the haul of presents we'd bring home from that snowy wonderland.

It was always the same, though. We rarely got what we really wanted. Everyone gave gifts in our family, and many were aunts and uncles we hardly knew. They certainly didn't know us, and that was apparent in their choice of gifts: a bright article of clothing we wouldn't be caught dead wearing, a book or two on subjects that held no interest for us, and those bizarre packages from distant relatives that we knew were thrown together in haste at the local discount store the previous day. These were a weird combination of low-priced, easy to find crap, like scarves and hats, paddle balls, and portable Chinese checker sets. My brother and I would exchange a knowing glance, then smile politely and say thank you. We stashed them under the upstairs beds, never to be seen again.

The truth was that our parents didn't have much money. The trip to Vermont every other year was more than they could afford, and my mother's parents, I learned later, often pitched in to help. But they weren't well off, either. I didn't understand it at that time, but those trips *were* the Christmas gifts. The rest was just decoration.

I looked down at my blinking cursor, now missing the brother I'd lost in a car accident shortly after our last trip back east, and closed my eyes. Maybe Loretta could help. I made us grilled cheese sandwiches because that's her favorite food. We have an agreement that when we're working, we don't talk. We sit just across the room, facing each other, our desks cluttered with books and printed pages that align to whatever project we're involved with. We don't disturb each other's concentration. And though I am prone to writing in twenty or thirty minute bursts interspersed with walking the dog, doing laundry, or surfing the web, Loretta can go off somewhere in her head and work with absolute focus for six, eight, even ten hour stretches. She'll suddenly burst out of her chair and go to the kitchenette, which is simply a counter on the other side of the room, and gulp down two glasses of water. Or she'll race into the bathroom and pee off a morning's pot of tea, the tinkling sound going on forever. Then she'll plop down in front of her computer and be gone again. I've learned not to talk to her during these pit stops. She isn't out of the zone. She's just letting it simmer for a second.

But the grilled cheese worked, and soon she was sitting back in her chair, her glasses on her head amidst the disarray of curls, staring at me. "You're making two of those. Right?"

"Oh, you want one?" I said. "Sure. But only if you'll go down to the beach with me afterward."

She looked out the window at the steady rain. "Okay."

Our dog Spike whined at the door as we ate our sandwiches. I've never really understood how he knows when we're planning to go for a walk. He'll lay curled on his bed under my desk for hours, but as soon as I have the *idea* to go out, he's at the door. No words, no movement, but some sort of mental telepathy prevails.

Oregon doesn't have much in the way of seashells. Maybe it's the rough coastline. Perhaps nothing can survive the battering of surf on rocks whole and intact. All I know is that we find fragments of clam shells, quarter sand dollars, dead jelly fish, and long whips of sea kelp, but it's a rare day that we find anything whole. Loretta spent her childhood Christmases in Cocoa Beach, Florida. She's from Arkansas, originally. When she moved in with me ten or so years ago, she had a ratty sofa, a laundry basket, some clothes, and an extensive seashell collection. She'd found each and every one of them herself, and they ranged from brightly colored and perfect to petrified and calcified broken shards. They were symbolic, like savings toward her dream to live near the ocean. Occasionally, I find a seashell at a second-hand shop or Goodwill and I toss it out onto the sand when she's not looking. She has the eyes of a hawk. She can spot the one linoleum tile that's installed backwards in seconds. She can read a street sign from blocks away. And she scans the beach like radar.

Today I had a full sand dollar, and a nice big one. I'd gotten it for fifty cents, but that's not the point. The point is that she found it in the foaming surf and jumped up and down like a little kid, holding it high in the air. It was a victory.

I sometimes think she knows it's me. But she hasn't said anything, so maybe not.

"Look," she said, breathless, her hand flat, the dollar resting on her palm. "It's huge."

"Wow," I said, picking it up. "That's a nice one."

"The storm must have brought it in." She looked out at the sea, raindrops sticking to her eyelashes, the hood of her raincoat drawn tight around her face.

It's true that storms bring in treasures from the sea, but lately all we'd been finding was garbage from the Japanese tsunami. They have a lot of Styrofoam over there it seems.

"I need your help with this project," I said, as we walked northward, the wind in our faces. "I don't know the first thing about gift giving."

"Maybe you should do a little poll," she said. "Ask some friends about their customs and what-not."

"Okay, I'll start with you."

She grimaced.

"Tell me about gift giving in your family." It wasn't like I didn't already know, but I wanted to hear her describe it. I'd spent a holiday or two with her family in Little Rock. Her sister is an architect there, and their parents live in a nice two-story house on a pleasant, tree-lined street near a shopping mall. We saw a lot of movies when we were in Arkansas.

"What do you want me to tell you? You know we're really bad at this. Remember when I tried to get everyone to dispense with buying each person a gift and just donate to charity, instead?"

I did remember it. It was a disaster. The idea had a lot of merit, I thought. Who needed another sweater that didn't fit, or hand massager that would languish in a drawer. If we were going to spend the money, why not actually put it use where it was needed like feeding the hungry. But her older brother, who lives in San Diego with his wife and two kids, flipped out about it and created a huge rift in the family. He refused to go along, stating that he liked the gift giving custom and he was going to give gifts even if no one else did. He was also the only one who could really afford it. It put their parents in an awkward position and they ended up giving money to charity *and* giving gifts to everyone.

"I hate spending my hard-earned money on things for Donny's kids," she said. "Then finding them broken or lying in the yard. They have no gratitude. They don't even say thank you."

One year Loretta bought them each science kits in colorful boxes for Christmas. She'd actually put some work into picking them out, making sure they were age appropriate, and she was excited to see them open the gifts. Donny's kids were about five and seven, maybe a little older. Ashley opened hers first. She looked at it and tossed it down into the pile of wrapping paper and asked what other presents were for her. When Loretta's mother insisted that Ashley show everyone what she got from Aunt Loretta, Ashley held them up and said, "Just some dumb magic tricks."

That was it for Loretta. She hasn't bought the kids another gift since. She started sending the family a basket of nuts and cheese for Christmas, instead. Something over-priced, over-wrapped, and over-preserved that she finds on the internet and has shipped direct. She bitches about the cost for days each time she does it, too. I've come to hate holiday shopping, even though we don't actually leave the house.

"I'm not really the one to ask about this," she said. She threw a tennis ball for Spike and he raced down the beach, upsetting a flock of seagulls that were huddled against the rain. Spike is golden retriever-mix and he's got a soft coat that smells like mildew all the time, even when he's clean and dry. We adopted him from the pound in Portland after we'd moved to the beach, and as soon as we understood that that smell never really goes away, no matter how hard you work at it, we got him his own bed. We buy more baking soda than actual bakers because it's the only thing that seems to keep the smell down to a tolerable level.

The walk back to the house is steep, and we always peel layers of clothing off on the way. As I chugged up the hill, staring at Loretta's attractive backside, I decided to write about holiday giving the way everyone believes it's supposed to be, rather than the way it actually is. Inside, I pounded out a segment that suggested different classes of gifts, such as non-personal fruit baskets and cookies versus more personal items like razors and clothing, and how determining what to give should be based on your familiarity with the person. For business purposes, it's always best to go with non-personal items with non-specific sentiments: *Happy Holidays from fill-in-the-blank organization.*

Loretta likes to be spanked. When she first told me that she wanted me to spank her, I didn't know what to do. I'm a nice guy. I was raised to never hit a woman, and this seemed a bit too close to assault at first. But she has a great ass, and I like having her stretched across my lap, pants down, wearing a tight little thong. Those round, firm cheeks are amazing to look at and to play with. And once I got over my initial resistance, I got into it. In fact, I found a website that sells all sorts of spanking paraphernalia, including books of short stories that aren't exactly literature, but we never make it all the way through the story, anyway. What I really learned was that this was a *thing*. And a lot of people enjoyed it. So I threw all in with her little sexual fantasy, and I recently bought some stuff to make it more fun.

Now I didn't just bring the box in and plop it down on my desk. I told her I was going into town for a cup of concentration at the local coffee shop, which wasn't a lie. I'd been tracking the package, and I intercepted the UPS driver in town on the day it was due to arrive—Neskowin is a really tiny town. All you have to do is sit in front of the general store, which is also the coffee shop, and watch for the driver. He'll invariably stop there anyway. I told him that the road to my house was washed out and that I knew he'd be coming. It was a plausible statement because the single most frequent naturally occurring disruption in western Oregon is landslides. He was grateful that I saved him the aggravation.

When I got back home, I slipped in and went to the bedroom to change out of my wet clothes. Loretta was in her writing zone, and I could have set the place on fire and she would have kept working. But a doorbell, that's different. That would have brought her to the surface. Anyway, in the bedroom, I carefully unwrapped the new items, hooking the hand-restraints to the headboard. I placed the new whip gently on the bed and took the cardboard box out to the recycling. You have to go through the bedroom to get to the bathroom in our house. It's one of those charming little aspects of coastal living. Most of these cottages were designed by men with good building skills, but no sense of feng shui. Loretta broke for a pit stop twice that afternoon, walking through the bedroom, past the scene of her coming punishment, without even noticing. I have to wonder, though, if her psyche took it in, even if her conscious mind didn't. The wait for her to comprehend it made me horny beyond all reason. I couldn't work. My dick was hard, and hurting against my jeans. I changed into sweats and wandered back and forth from my desk to the window, right in her line of vision, sporting a hard-on. Nothing.

Finally, I had reached the end of my rope, and I asked her if she would come see something. I was firm. It was important. The house needed a serious repair, here in the… bedroom. She's a sharp girl and her antennae went up at the mention of the bedroom. She homed in on my hard-on instantly and sat back in her chair, smiled, and shook her head.

"I'm working, babe."

"Not any more, you aren't," I informed her with stern perseverance. The thing about women who like to be spanked is that your assumptions about the rest of their personality can be dead wrong. Loretta is a tough minded, independent woman. She doesn't need me, not in the sense of needing a man to take care of her. If she thought I was punishing her for real, she'd castrate me. It's fantasy, and as such, I have to be careful about the way I play it.

"You've been very bad," I said, and worked to keep a straight face.

"Have I?" she asked, one eyebrow raised.

"Enough talk. Get in the bedroom now." I stood in front of her desk expectantly.

She eyed me as if to size up my ability to make her, then acquiesced to my demand.

This isn't porn, so I'm not going into the details. This is about gift giving, and I think I gave Loretta a damn fine gift with those new toys. And I thought, this is the best part of gift giving. Getting it exactly right, and then getting to be part of the person's joy.

And it occurred to me, too, that it was pretty fucking selfish of Loretta's niece Ashley to treat her that way about the science kit. It's good she wasn't my daughter, because I would've taught that kid a lesson in gratitude.

Loretta's cheeks stay pink after sex. Her hair is often so tangled and crazy that the only way to tame it is a hot shower with a lot of conditioner. But she likes to walk around in her robe and sweats after sex, drinking cocoa with whiskey and humming. And I like to make her cocoa to keep her from taking a shower and returning to work. It usually means we're done working for the day, and those are the best days.

I tuned in our internet TV and found a documentary about mad cow disease, and we snuggled on the sofa with our cocoa.

Valentine's Day was coming up, and I'd been thinking about in context to this project. I had been struggling with what to write, or whether to include it at all. It seemed to me and my male friends like an elaborate game in which only the female knows the rules. It was the fastball you took in the ribs each year. Loretta and I had had some Valentine missteps. The first year she said she didn't care about the holiday and not to bother doing anything. But she wasn't my first girlfriend, and I understood that to mean I had better get her something nice, and I had better surprise her. Maybe the reason I fell in love with Loretta is because she had meant what she'd said. But I didn't know that then, and when I presented her with a dozen roses, she looked worried, and then a little angry.

"I didn't get you anything," she said.

"You didn't have to."

"But you got me something."

And we had a long night of weird feelings. It didn't turn out at all like I thought it would. We repeated that weird scenario the following year, but with a slightly less expensive gift. Finally, she said, "Mitch, I really don't like Valentine's Day. *Gift* and *obligatory* are diametrically opposed. If someone is telling you that you have to do it, it isn't really a gift."

Loretta and I got married on Valentine's Day four years after we met. People tell us all the time that we're so romantic. But it was an uprising, a revolt against the establishment. We were taking that day back so it could never be anything more than our anniversary, which we understood better how to celebrate.

"I was thinking about your project," she said, muting the television. "I got the invitation for Alice and Jason's wedding yesterday."

"Oh?" I set my half-drunk cocoa down, wishing it was coffee. This was an area of gift giving that I had been putting off thinking about. I'd researched and read about the easier ones, and had decided to stick to the standard wisdom as doled out by tradition. But the wedding gift, and its kin, the baby shower gift? These were my least favorite situations.

Loretta pulled out the wedding invitation and read it aloud. At the very end, she looked at me, a mischievous smile at her lips. "Registered at *Pottery Barn*," she said.

I dropped my head back against the sofa. "I am SO the wrong person to be writing about this shit."

"Pottery Barn," she repeated, looking around our cozy cottage with its second-hand furniture and mismatched colors.

"Why do I hate the idea of a registry so much?" I said. "I mean, really, if you think about it, it makes it easy. You get them exactly what they want and you can do it in twenty minutes."

"I'll tell you why," Loretta said, putting her mug down on the water-stained coffee table. "Because it says three things: 1. We expect you to buy us a gift. 2. We don't trust you to pick out what we want. And 3. We'll know exactly how much you spent."

She is so articulate. I love her.

"That's marketing genius," I told her.

"It's bullshit!"

"You should write this project," I said.

"I'd get fired."

We watched TV for a while, and I thought about the concept of gift registries. Loretta was right. But the part I was stuck on was why were we obliged to give gifts at all? It wasn't like Alice and Jason were just starting out. They were in their 30s. Alice had been married once before. When they merged their households a couple of years earlier, they sold a sofa and a queen sized bed, which we now owned. Hadn't the idea of gift giving come from a time when the young couple was just starting out and needed basic stuff like a frying pan and a butter churn? Alice is a CPA and Jason is a computer programmer. Between them they likely make triple what Loretta and I do. Did they really need plates and flatware from their unemployed writer friends?

The project dragged. I took a lot of walks into town for coffee, and the whole thing was becoming a drudgery on par with Christmas shopping itself. One morning I slept late, which I sometimes do when I don't want to face a project. By the time I rolled out of bed it was ten o'clock and Loretta had already been down to the beach with Spike. It was sunny, and the shimmer from the surf was so bright it hurt my eyes. I slammed around, tossing my papers and noisily cleaning my desk for a while, then I stripped the bed and started the laundry. I was in no mood to work, and when I can't work, I'm in no mood to do anything else, either. I pulled on my jeans and a hoodie and told her I was going to walk downtown and get some coffee. Loretta drinks only tea—green tea, and only Iron Goddess of Mercy. She never comes along for coffee.

She just looked at me over her glasses. I wondered why she was being pissy and started for Spike's leash. That's when I saw it. It was a brand new coffee press made of copper and glass. It was just big enough for a really fine cup of coffee— nothing left over to get cold. And she'd provided the really fine coffee, too. My favorite local brew, Flag & Wire, which has to be special ordered at the general store. It had been sitting there on the counter in plain sight as I threw my little temper tantrum.

I picked up the beans and smelled them. Heaven. I gave her a look of apology. Words can often be meaningless, especially to writers.

"You're sometimes an ass," she said. "But I still love you." And she returned to her work.

After I made myself that really fine cup of coffee, I decided enough with the procrastination. I was going to finish this project and get it out of my life forever. I thought about all my angst around giving and all I had read on the internet and at the library about the different customs. I wanted to say something profound. Impart some amazing wisdom to the gift-giving masses—something about how receiving a gift isn't about *you*, but about how the person who's giving it *sees* you. But I couldn't quite get words around that idea. They sounded trite or sentimental, and it would only be lost in translation, anyway. So I detailed how the gift registry works, and how it makes the whole business so much easier and happier for everyone. I resisted the urge to substitute "happier" with "poorer." After all, who was I to say? I don't know shit about gift giving.

SUE WILLIAM SILVERMAN

If *Love Is Here Every Day!*

The girl lurks under the Jersey
Shore boardwalk, black leather, hair
braiding her to the pillar,
where this promise is sprayed.

The Ferris wheel circles
the moon, the boardwalk
splinters with smutty
kisses. A camera captures

her acquiescence and defiance.
She reads a novel, fading
into fiction and darkness, her
mouth pink cotton candy.

A man's tissue-paper-thin
breath trembles in
expensive moonlight. His
luminous shirt shines

like a star in wind piercing
a sallow sky. She swallows
a mouthful of light.
Tail-finned

cars   speed   toward
Atlantic foam, salt bruises
her tongue. The season
is over. The girl's wan

smile is a last carousel ride,
wood horses distorted
in mirrors. She'd translate
her body back into its own

language, if only she could.

First appeared in *Cultural Weekly*, Nov. 25, 2015

SIERRA SITZES

The Baptism of Anna Spence

I. Do Not Gratify the Desires of the Flesh

KURT AND I START PREMARITAL COUNSELING because it's the church's policy and, with the effort to give up sex, we now masturbate too much. Any sort of lust, we're told, is natural, but not ideal, and there are ways to fight it. Fight temptation. Fight, we're told, by not using the Internet if we feel tempted. To get up and exercise if we feel tempted. Keep each other accountable if we feel tempted. But mostly just pray. Brother Lars tells us the same applies to sex and he strongly suggests for us to stop living together until the wedding. "Strongly suggests" equals "Too many fuck-ups in these next sixteen weeks before the wedding and I have the right not to marry you."

He tells us he won't condone lost causes, but we have something that keeps us from that group. Something he calls 'genuine compassion.'

Or love. But in the first two weeks of counseling no one uses that word.

Kurt tells me later he doesn't want to be outed as a lost cause and he packs two weeks worth of clothes and moves in with his mother. It's only four months, he reminds me. And he's right. Four months. We have four months to make the wedding night as special as possible and to make up for the last year of living together.

On top of these three-way sessions with the pastor, I've been going to one-on-one, hour and a half to two hour long sessions in which I relay my preconceived stereotypes about being Baptist which Brother Lars either confirms or denies.

The majority of the time is spent confirming with "buts."

Yes, Baptist doctrine prohibits dance, but not necessarily all dance. Just dance that conveys any sort of sexual movement. And any sort of dancing done in the church.

Yes, Baptist doctrine prohibits female leadership, but only leading the men. He cites verses in one of the Corinthians and says the church is open to female leadership, but with other women and children.

Yes, Baptist doctrine prohibits drinking alcohol, but there is no "but' to follow this. The only thing alcohol leads to, he says, is another kind of impurity. Any other kind of impurity.

I'm finding it difficult to disagree.

Kurt suggests I try to find someone to sublease while he's gone and I call Charlise who just moved back from a failed internship in Kansas City and needs a place to live. I move my desk and bookshelves from my office so she doesn't have to sleep in the living room. She pays half the rent. She thanks me repeatedly for the opportunity. She praises the not-summer wedding. She'll have all her stuff out the week before we're married, she says.

It's easy for us to fall back into our roommate routine. The night after she moves her stuff in we open a bottle of wine and start the remembers.

Remember meeting in Spanish 101? Remember how I hated you? I ask her if she remembers desperately asking me if I needed a roommate the next year. She remembers me saying yes without hesitation.

She asks me if I'm really into the whole God thing now and I tell her yes, of course. After she passes out on the couch I pray. I pray because I'm drunk with someone for the first time in a long time. I pray to fall asleep and to keep my hands to myself.

There's a lack of musk now, even though most of Kurt's possessions are still here. At first, he was staying the night, but after two transgressions he only visits. Leaves around midnight with a kiss on the forehead and reassurance that we're doing the right thing.

I talk to Charlise with schoolgirl confidence that what we're doing is right and she is inspired by my resolve. This week, she says, she's only going to drink three nights. She starts coming into my room in the morning without knocking, wanting to talk about how refreshed she is waking up without the weight of a bottle of wine, about some new guy and a new escapade she feels isn't worth her time. I hide under the covers sans pants and fight the territorial aggression that comes with not coming.

One night Kurt calls close to three in the morning. He tells me he wants to come over, but he won't. Tells me he wants to talk dirty, but he won't. He wants to touch himself, but he won't. He had a wet dream a couple nights ago and he feels guilty about it.

I pretend to be supportive and part of me is proud we'll have something to talk to Brother Lars about on Tuesday night. Brother Lars is proud that we, as a couple have taken legitimate steps to conquering temptation. Our compassion has not only pushed Kurt out of the apartment, but us into a better direction.

I decide I will neglect to tell Kurt in this moment, or Brother Lars in any of our sessions, doctrinal, premarital or otherwise, that I couldn't keep my hands off myself every morning this week. I decide not to talk about how there's just something about secret stroking under sheets. Worn cotton on thighs. Secret moments only God sees.

Instead, I listen while Kurt talks about hailing Mary.

I ask if he knows how to, to hail Mary.

He tells me no. He's never prayed to the saints, either. He's not sure how that works, but that's why he thinks about it. Different religions keep him preoccupied. I make a joke about thinking about Mother Mary to keep thy hands away from thyself and I tell him how I know nothing about Catholic doctrine, either. Nothing other than that they drink actual wine out of one cup vs. Welches out of plastic shot glasses.

He laughs. Tells me this is why he loves me, because I can make light out of heavy situations, and he falls asleep. I listen to his deep breathing, try to pray, and then touch myself. Thinking about musk. About breathing. About Mother Mary.

II. You Are Fearfully and Wonderfully Made

I tell Brother Lars about the panic attacks I (used to) have during sex. I tell him that's how I knew Kurt was "the one," because he understood. He understands. He'd hold me until it was over. Help me breathe. Brother Lars tells me good. It's good to have a partner for support, but God should be my rock. He tells me my reactions have nothing to do with being raped at sixteen, or depression, or PTSD, or all the other things the other counselors told me when I was under a haze of Prozac and Xanax. It's because, he says, the Holy Spirit was convicting me about sinning.

I don't verbally disagree, but I'm praying while he's talking. Asking God if it's true. If the years of counseling and therapy were all for not and I feel nothing that tells me I was wrong. Brother Lars keeps lecturing and I keep nodding and listening and I think about seeing my stomach hang down the last time Kurt and I did it like dogs and how Kurt, with good intentions, tells me he likes a curvy woman. He likes that I'm soft. Runs his hands lightly over my new rolls and stretch marks with more compassion than I've ever seen in anyone and I believe him.

Thirty pounds put on in the last year and he says it's all right. He's hoping my conversion will keep me from drinking. From indulging. It will, I think. I'm hoping for weight lost.

My baptism is scheduled in two weeks and this Sunday we watch two vacation bible school kids get dunked in a glorified bathtub behind the pulpit with a Plexiglas front, their white baptism robes billow in the water, stirred by the Holy Spirit. I'll be in that tank soon, billowing with champagne, with cabernet sauvignon, with margaritas, citrus vodka and spiced rum from a flask.

Kurt's arm is behind me, not around my shoulders but on the back of the pew I'm leaning on. I feel its heat and imagine the way it looks underneath his shirtsleeves. Tight. Not as tight as before he gave up self stroking. Not as tight as the bodies of the other women in his life.

I tell Brother Lars I hate my body. I hate that I can feel the new weight in my shoes. I tell him about the new diet I'm on: twelve hundred calories a day. I tell him I've put myself on it because if I don't, I'll be carrying an extra twenty pounds in another month or two, fifteen in the next week.

He tells me I'm fearfully and wonderfully made and that these thoughts I have aren't from God, but from our adversary.

Am I my own adversary? I ask. And he tells me if I'm not careful, guarded, the devil can use me, too.

I pray and ask God to help me love my body and then tell Kurt what Brother Lars said, that I need to lose weight to keep the devil from using me. Kurt doesn't question it. Instead he says that for the wedding, less than ten weeks away, we'll start cooking dinner together more, nothing but whole grains and vegetables and lean, white meat.

He asks me questions to confirm that I'm not drinking as much and I tell him, right. That Charlise keeps asking me to go out with her and I tell her no. Which is true.

He doesn't know that on the nights he doesn't come over and I don't feel like going out, the two of us make drinks like we used to with whiskey and schnapps and pretend to be six years younger living in our dorm room. I will never tell him about how, after four drinks, we feel suffocated and take our clothes off, how we sit naked on the furniture he and I bought with our children's safety in mind talking about our celebrity sex lists. I will never tell him about the questions she asks me about him, questions that range anywhere from the size of his cock to his belief in God. That I stand firm in my new-found faith, but I acknowledge that her doubts have a lot of merit, too.

During our one-on-ones, Brother Lars asks if I'm still struggling with drinking, and I confess I am, but not as much anymore. I've gotten really good at praying about it. What I don't tell him, and what I mean, is that I pray the most when I'm drunk. He asks me how I feel about my body and I confess I hate it less. That some mornings (mornings, I'll never tell him, I resist the temptation of feeling Kurt's hands in my head) I look at myself in the mirror and I think, this is all right. I'm fearfully and wonderfully made and I'm more than okay. And I tell him about the other mornings, too, not that they outweigh the others three to one, but that I slip back into my old train of thought and spend forty five minutes or more counting the new rolls on my stomach and back and the stretch marks that accompany them.

III. Your Body Is A Temple

Brother Lars, thank God, doesn't think I'm actually an alcoholic. He thinks that my habits lean toward its development, but really it's not bad enough to seek treatment.

He tells me he won't lie to me, that he's a little worried about my emotional reliance on it, but he has faith. It is a good sign, my concern, which goes beyond my spiritual convictions and reaches into my personal health. He tells me anecdotes about previous converts who went through rehab, who he recommended treatment through AA, and he tells me I'm not there. Yet. He tells me he's praying that I'll find a way through the drinking, that five nights will be narrowed down to two will be narrowed down to none.

When he asks me why I think I drink I tell him out of habit, not that I'm trying to forget sex with Kurt or sex with myself, or the "sex" when I was sixteen.

The week before my baptism he and Kurt have a long, drawn out conversation about the wedding plans. Brother Lars is disappointed we won't be conducting our wedding reception in the church. Kurt tries to explain that, although that's what he would prefer, most of my family would refuse to show up if we didn't have the luxury of an open bar. Brother Lars hopes it won't be too big a temptation for me and Kurt tells him, of course not, that I haven't had a drink in weeks. That I wouldn't dream of getting drunk on our special day.

While both men talk for me I think about Charlise and I and how we took shots five years ago before our oral exam for Spanish 401. How, despite our being obviously intoxicated, we did well and our Spanish Professor invited us out with some of his Peruvian friends the next night for drinks to celebrate our finishing the class with an A.

I imagine Kurt in that bar, watching me and Charlise attempt to keep up with their conversational Spanish. In a dark corner, he's hailing Mary, holding a rosary over his head, away from His as the bartender pours us another round of shots of cinnamon whiskey. They were bought by Brother Lars who takes a shot with us and introduces himself to me for the first time. I imagine he's the type of drunk that's happy to see everyone, who flirts with girls and when he is rejected, takes it with good grace. Drunkenly he slurs a joke, *When fishing with a Baptist, how do you keep him from drinking all your beer?* Kurt has come out from the corner, his hands still above his head clutching beads, and he shrugs. *Invite another Baptist.* We all laugh. We all take another shot of grape-flavored vodka from plastic communion cups.

They ask me, did you hear us?

No. I confess to zoning out.

We're proud of you.

Brother Lars reminds us that he had faith in us. From the beginning. There's so much 'compassion' between us.

The night before my baptism I get drunk by myself off the whiskey Charlise keeps on top of the refrigerator and throw out the empty wine bottles on my nightstand. I remember the morning before my first one-on-one with Brother Lars and how later, with a wine dried tongue, I asked him about the evils of alcohol.

I invite Charlise to my service hoping that her presence will alleviate, if not cancel out, being in that baptismal with Brother Lars while the 10:30 congregation watches. She declines with a half-joke about how, if she walked through the threshold of a church, she or it would spontaneously combust.

I tell her that wouldn't happen. Especially if she joined me in the baptismal. Later that night she meets up with some friends and doesn't ask me to go with her.

Drunkenly, I make toasts in my empty apartment.

To the cleansing of sin!

To Kurt at his mother's!

To the weight washed clean by a public profession of faith!

I have a small collection of wine corks. I throw them away, one by one, holding them up to my nose and trying to remember the wine that made the smell. On one it is printed 'Avoid beer.'

What about grappa from a chalice? Grain from plastic shot glasses?

The morning of my baptism, I find two cigarette boxes in the tampon box in one of the church's bathrooms. For a moment I'm tempted to tear them apart and flush them. What if they're found and someone thinks they're mine?

I'm relieved when I remember that, oh yes, of all the things I've confessed to Brother Lars the last eight weeks, not once have I mentioned a tobacco problem. He'll know it's not me. Especially if he knew about last night. About the beer I drank out of spite when I saw that wine cork. How I touched myself and never came trying to remember Kurt's hands in my head. Came when I thought about Charlise naked and lounging in my armchair.

The choir stops singing and the water is lukewarm on my ankles. Thighs. Waist. It does nothing to encourage or discourage.

Brother Lars wraps his arms around my shoulders. Without moving my lips I beg him to pull me back. Pull me under. I want to be submerged in the Luke-warmed water.

As usual, no one is sitting in the two front rows in the sanctuary, but Kurt and his family sit in the third and fourth smiling, watching the water push the white robes against my used-to-be thinish body.

I stop looking out over the sanctuary, at Brother Lars. Instead I imagine God rendering the congregation blind just long enough for him to leave the baptismal and pull bottles of Maker's Mark and Jameson from behind the podium and pour them into the water. An invisible moment only God sees. I imagine that when the light is lifted the congregation thinks it sees urine through the Plexiglas. I imagine it staining our robes, my new body's stretch marks. And then without warning I'm pulled backwards and drink deep. One last drink before I resurface in the name of the Father, and of the Son, and of the Holy Ghost. Forever and ever. Amen.

Andy Smart

Uphill with Lady

She says *rose quartz* and I kick my boot
over the pink geology underfoot.
She says *coyote* and I shuffle-lumber my eyes
away from her and to the woods—columnar trees,
cobwebs, a fine mist of seen breath—
but no creeping myth trickster.
She says *stop* and the fever of the universe boils
into sweatlets in my beard.
She says *come.* I embrace the angel dust
between her body and mine. Contact. A moment,
only. She says *go*, and the fever of the universe
breaks. I pick a flower and say 'gift.' Dig up
a stone and say 'precious.'
She says *beautiful nothing*.

Debbie Theiss

Second Chance?

She refuses to pick up the phone.
The name she recognizes, her son.
It's too late for a call, really.
Rehash the story? It's been done.

Must look ahead, not reflect
or allow him to draw her in. A
drug bust, a chronic relapse,
back in prison to serve again.

The cigarette burns, glows and smolders.
A shrouded, gray-filtered cloud
settles over the phone's blinking light.
One message is left, no doubt.

Inhales the smoke, sweet and bitter.
She presses the button to play.
His voice, both throaty and strained
asks forgiveness, "What do you say?"

Michaella Thornton

After the Final No

"WE SHOULD TAKE a naked lap," Paul said, pointing to the high school track before us. He was slightly drunk, and we were sitting on the bleachers, retelling old stories. The rehearsal dinner was over, the one where he, at the end of the night, had grabbed my hand when I came out of the bathroom, a secular Wailing Wall, an everyday space containing so many secret griefs.

Of course, he hadn't noticed I had been crying.

We had been Spartans a lifetime ago – he, a budding chemist and track-and-field star; me, a girl in love with Math Club and an alchemy of words. I immediately shook my head "no" at his crazy suggestion and pulled my down coat tighter.

"It's the dead of January," I stammered.

"So what?"

I knew I would probably never see Paul after his wedding to the woman no one could reasonably hate: big, brown eyes and a Southern drawl – sweeter and quicker than molasses. Why did he ask me here when he had Kate? Why did I agree to this when I knew he would soon be states away, nurturing a marriage and a family?

But on those bleachers, I relented and finally said yes. Yes like Wallace Stevens wrote about after the final no: *If the rejected things, the things denied, / Slid over the western cataract, yet one, / One only, one thing that was firm, even.* Yes to an intimacy far greater than nostalgic yearning or the easy gratification of just one night.

As we threw off our clothes and raced towards the track, I knew I would let Paul go without a fight.

I led Paul for the first 100 meters, both of us without a stitch – breasts and penis flopping, buttocks pumping, knees high with soft bellies bouncing. My lead was falsely earned. Paul took in an eyeful of ample ass before his victory lap, before he regretted we had never dated in high school, before he realized my form wasn't just an accumulation of thrift-store cardigans and well-worn jeans. Of course, I thought, he wouldn't regret that there was no us, no me. He would race me but marry her. They were going to live in Baltimore, maybe see John Waters, have a baby, and suck out the sweet, white meat of blue crab.

Not me. Years ago I had given up meat and the prospect of marriage, became an accountant, and sang bluesy Big Mama Thornton songs in the shower. Sometimes my on-again, off-again boyfriend, Bill, would come over. A placeholder for social gatherings and my libido. We had sex while listening to public radio, content in our boredom. Bill didn't think it odd that a 30-something woman would meet her estranged childhood friend by the bleachers of their old high school like a bad cover of a John Cougar Mellencamp song.

The morning after our naked race, I sat next to Bill at the church in a navy wool dress and pearls. Paul and Kate kissed amid the firelight with plenty of tongue. We held sparklers in our gloved hands and danced to Etta James and James Brown. There was cannoli instead of cake, and I was annoyed. Cake was far more satisfying than cannoli. The pick-your-favorite dessert-in-lieu-of-wedding-cake trend was tiresome.

As Bill and I two-stepped to Bonnie Raitt's "Thing Called Love," I kept thinking about the ancient Spartans' naked triumph, their steely resolve, and unfettered footraces. I thought about the blues. Of the lives that were hummed, never sang, a distant throbbing held under one's tongue until the possibility of desire is muffled and quieted by the throat, the stomach, the womb, the heart.

Neither of us ever mentioned that night at the track. Paul (really Kate) and I still exchange Christmas cards and share friends on Facebook. But it is hard not to think about the sting of frozen polyurethane on our feet, the wintry wind encasing our bodies in gooseflesh, and the denied lust of not yet, not probably, not ever. No.

Robert Vivian

Clouds Above The River

LIFTING MY FACE, lifting everyone's, even the long ago vanished faces of the dead, holy drifting, naked and alone with all there is, towering and sheer and full of radical freefall, lightening, thunder, and ozone, the voices of ancestors talking about the river in murmurs I can't quite hear as the river moves through me and I through it, wading to get where I am, gazing above the river to the clouds and how the trees seem to know in their swaying something about living and dying then living again as the river sparkles here and there in perfect diadems and the bubble line runs out over a seam and what wildness beneath the surface and I half man and three-fourths water as the clouds show me the way home which is always nowhere and I am buoyant and tired and do not wish to speak but listen with every molecule of water to the living ache of beauty all around me and how the clouds above the river make the water dark then light again and I in these shifting hues divine my place among the stones and fishes as somehow part of them and how I can drink and wash my face, my hands, my life and the river will take the sweat and tears away, the blood and grime and the ancestors know but do not say for there is nothing to say because it has been spoken once for all of us and the current pushes hard against my hips for it has the world to save and would drown me in its wake without malice or mercy as I see through to the clarity of things and how there is skinny water maybe 200 yards away and there I will be able to rest and lift my gaze to the clouds again which may by then have already passed away, silent hymns and ghost traces, breath above the earth that provides all breathing, even little brother sparrow and belted kingfisher, even a slow and quiet stepper like me who's afraid to make a sound in this wide-awake kingdom of water and wind.

Jan Way

Short Shots

Rain on the old pond
Frog at edge
A big snake approaches

…….

A Janus moon
Half fulfills us
With dark or light

…….

The black ball drops
Janis Joplin sings alone
Death filters her screams

……

African art mask
Indian art mask
Modern ego mask

…….

Guardian angels
Special ops
In hostile territory

…….

We are called to help unbind one another.

Contributor's Notes

John Abernathy is a graduate of Vermont College of Fine Arts' Writing program and Savannah College of Art & Design's Film and Television program. He teaches Composition at Arkansas State University and occasionally publishes coloring books and children's literature. John does not have any children but he does sunburn very easily. For *You're an Abernathy* he imagined an older, grumpier version of himself giving advice to a younger, more hopeful version. It was therapeutic.

C. D. Albin was born and reared in West Plains, Missouri. He earned a Doctor of Arts in English from the University of Mississippi and has taught for many years at Missouri State University – West Plains, where he founded and edits *Elder Mountain: A Journal of Ozarks Studies*. His stories, poems, and reviews have appeared in a number of periodicals, including *Arkansas Review*, *Cape Rock*, *Georgia Review*, *Harvard Review*, *Natural Bridge*, and *Slant*.

Kelli Allen's work has appeared in numerous journals and anthologies in the US and internationally. She is a four-time Pushcart Prize nominee. She is currently a Professor of Humanities and Creative Writing at Lindenwood University. Allen gives readings and teaches workshops throughout the US. Her full-length poetry collection, *Otherwise, Soft White Ash*, from John Gosslee Books (2012) was nominated for the Pulitzer Prize. www.kelli-allen.com

Laura Baird has been a finalist in a Third Coast poetry contest. She's published in *Body* (Prague), *Canyon Voices*, *The Cortland Review*, *Numero Cinq*, *The Café Review*, *Sense Magazine*, and *em:me*. She is currently working on her first book of poetry as well as a chapbook manuscript. Laura lives in Montgomery, Alabama.

She is a psychotherapist in private practice for 20 years and mother to two daughters.

Ian Bodkin is a writer. He is the author of the poetry collection *Every Word Was Once Drunk,* and a collaborative book of poetry with poet Lee Busby, *Fingertip Scriptures.* He also writes a continuing comic book with artist William Bennett, set in the post apocalyptic future known simply as *The Savage Lyrics.* He lives with his wife and son just north of the James River in Richmond, VA.

Nikki Boss lives in New England with her husband, children, and too many animals. She is a current MFA candidate at Vermont College of Fine Arts. Her work can be found several places online, and she's still holding onto pipe dreams of writing fame.

Michael Brasier's work has appeared in *Crack the Spine, Fiction Southeast, Elder Mountain Journal, Sassafras Literary Magazine,* and *Paddle Shots: A River Pretty Anthology.* He received his Bachelor's in English from Missouri State University.

Karen W. Burton is a lifelong lover of words and rivers. These two loves combine often in her poetry and prose. She received her MFA from Lindenwood University, and her work has appeared in *Foliate Oak, Canyon Voices, The Lindenwood Review, What Not to Say (anthology),* and others. She is an adjunct professor at Maryville University in St. Louis.

Natalie Byers is a MFA candidate at Vermont College of Fine Arts. Her first chapbook, *The Great and Terrible* (ELJ Publications) was released in the fall of 2015. Other work has appeared in *Slipstream, foothill, Upstart,* and elsewhere.

Marcus Cafagña is the author of two poetry collections, *The Broken World*, which won the 1995 National Poetry Series, and most recently, *Roman Fever*. He is the Coordinator of the Creative Writing Program at Missouri State University.

Katch Campbell MSN, MFA is a poet, scientist, & mom living in the woods outside of Philadelphia. When she isn't driving her two teens about she is training for triathlons and working as a scientific writer for biopharm. It's a dichotomy. A recent grad from Vermont College of fine arts. Katch's work can also be found at *Zomagazine* and *Queenmobs*.

Barbara Siegel Carlson is the author of *Fire Road* (Dream Horse Press, 2013) and co-translator of *Look Back, Look Ahead, Selected Poems of Srečko Kosovel* (Ugly Duckling Presse, 2010). Her poetry and translations have appeared in *The Carolina Quarterly, New Ohio Review, Prairie Schooner, Avatar Review* and elsewhere. She has work forthcoming in *Salamander* and *Mid American Review*. She lives in Carver, MA.

Kitty Carpenter studied Professional Writing and Creative Writing at Missouri State University. She loves writing, billiards, entomology, and the occasional getaway to River Pretty.

Derek Cowsert is currently finishing his MFA in Nonfiction at The University of Missouri - Kansas City and teaching English at Missouri State University. He lives in Hollister, Missouri.

Chris Daniel Crabtree hails from Springfield, Missouri, and is currently a teaching assistant in the M.A program at Missouri State University where he studies creative writing. His work has appeared in such journals as *Midwestern Gothic, Sundog, Elder Mountain,* and *NEAT*. This is his 10th River Pretty.

Jordan Culotta is pursuing an undergrad at the University of Tennessee at Chattanooga where she has had the opportunity to learn from Richard Jackson. After she graduates in May, she will be taking a year off to travel and then participating in an MFA program. She is passionate about social justice, feminism, organic farming, and swimming in the river.

Kristen Cypret will graduate with her Masters in Romance Languages and Literatures at the University of Missouri, Kansas City in May of 2016. She is a 2012 graduate of Missouri State University – Springfield where she earned a B.A. in English/Creative Writing. Her poetry has appeared in the *Moon City Review and Elder Mountain: A Journal of Ozark Studies*.

Jim Daniels has taught creative writing at Carnegie Mellon since 1981. His recent books include *Birth Marks* (2013) and *Having a Little Talk with Capital P Poetry* (2011), poetry; *Eight Mile High* (2014), and *Trigger Man*, short fiction (2011). He has edited or co-edited four anthologies, including *Letters to America: Contemporary American Poetry on Race, and American Poetry: The Next Generation*. My poems have been featured on Garrison Keillor's "Writer's Almanac," in Billy Collins' *Poetry 180* anthologies, and Ted Kooser's "American Life in Poetry" series.

Carrie Dimino works in Kansas as a Writing Center person and lives in Missouri as a Mother person. After completing her B.A. in Creative Writing at he College of Santa Fe in New Mexico and before completing her Masters in Professional Writing, at UMKC, she worked as a Peace Corps volunteer in Ukraine. She prefers the in-between to the here or the there.

Gregory Donovan is the author of the newly published poetry collection, *Torn from the Sun* (Red Hen Press, 2015), and the earlier *Calling His Children Home*, which won the Devins Award for Poetry, along with poems, essays, and fiction published in

The Kenyon Review, American Poetry Review, TriQuarterly, Gulf Coast, Copper Nickel, Crazyhorse, and many other journals, as well as in a number of anthologies, including *Common Wealth: Contemporary Poets of Virginia* (University of Virginia Press, 2003). Donovan is a faculty member in the graduate creative writing program at Virginia Commonwealth University, where he has often served as the Director of Creative Writing, and he is Senior Editor of the internationally recognized online journal *Blackbird*.

Alta Leah Emrick: My serious writing career began after retirement. I love writing and have had many published articles and poems. Presently, I am a member of Springfield Writers Guild, Ozarks Chapter of American Christian Writers, and Poets & Friends, holding several offices. Book-wise, I have written: *A Turtle and a Snail Walked Into a Café* joke book, *Everyday Wisdom for Successful Living, Grandma's Alta Fables,* and *Surviving and Thriving With Only God's Love.* Currently working on a one-man play.

Brandon Funk is originally from Ozark County, Missouri. He received his MA in English from Missouri State University in 2004. He teaches, writes, and lives in Kansas City.

D. Gilson is the author of *I Will Say This Exactly One Time: Essays* (Sibling Rivalry, 2015); *Crush* (Punctum Books, 2014), with Will Stockton; *Brit Lit* (Sibling Rivalry, 2013); and *Catch & Release* (2012), winner of the Robin Becker Prize. He is Assistant Professor of English at Massachusetts College of Liberal Arts, and his work has appeared in *PANK, The Indiana Review, The Rumpus,* and as a notable essay in *Best American Essays*.

Hunter Hobbs is a senior at the University of Tennessee at Chattanooga. I am majoring in English, with a focus on creative writing, and minoring in Philosophy. The poets that I believe have most influenced my work are: Thomas James, Arthur

Rimbaud, James Tate, and--of course--Rick Jackson. I am planning to continue studying poetry at the graduate level, and I will hopefully begin working on my MFA in the coming Fall semester.

Jimmy Huff is a graduate of the Creative Writing program at Missouri State University. His work has been nominated for the Pushcart Prize.

Robert Hyers' work has appeared in a few places including *The Summerset Review* and *Saints and Sinners: Fiction From the Festival*. He teaches freshman and sophomore college writing in New Jersey and has been known to visit River Pretty Writers Retreat from time to time. "Bosom Buddies" was first read at the Spring 2013 River Pretty Writers Retreat and, before appearing in this anthology, was published in *Jonathon 09*. "Bosom Buddies" will also be included in Robert's first short story collection, *Spinning The Record*, which will be published this July by Lethe Press.

Elizabeth Hykes: "Hand Blown in Ohio" won the scholarship at River Pretty in spring 2015. Images were drawn from a family home where my grandmother and mother were born and raised in Western Pennsylvania, near where I was born and raised. I visited there with my great aunt, Effie Hope Croyle, summers as a child and loved that house. She, too, was born there and died there. Aunt Effie was a teacher, starting at age 17 in a one room country school house, and retiring sometime in the 1970's after teaching more than 50 years in the community around the house. The land was an original land grant from William Penn, and up until Aunt Effie's death, had never been bought, sold, or mortgaged. It is gone from us now. How I miss that house and those people.

Richard Jackson is the author of thirteen books of poems, most recently *Retrievals* (C&R Press, 2014), *Out of Place* (Ashland, 2014), *Resonancia* (Barcelona, 2014, translation of *Resonance* from Ashland, 2010), *Half Lives: Petrarchan Poems* (Autumn House, 2004), *Unauthorized Autobiography: New and Selected Poems* (Ashland, 2003), and *Heartwall* (UMass, Juniper Prize 2000), as well as four chapbook adaptations from Pavese and other Italian poets. His newest book, *Traversings*, co-written with Robert Vivian is due out in 2016.

Kelly Jolene studied Creative Writing at University of Tennessee at Chattanooga and currently resides in New Mexico. She attended River Pretty twice and hopes to become a regular. She didn't realize poetry was a pyramid scheme until it was too late.

Matthew Kimberlin is the founding editor of Suburban Diaspora. He earned his MA in English from Missouri State University. His fiction has appeared in Paddle Shots and Curbside Splendor's e-zine, and he has contributed to Unstuck, Rougarou, and Moon City Review.

Mary Knobbe lives in St. Louis with her family and assorted animals. Most of the time she's listening to rock 'n roll, reading a trashy romance novel or writing down her inner monologue.

Timothy Leyrson received his MA from Missouri State University in 2013, and his MFA from University of Missouri-Kansas City in 2015 as a Durwood fellow. He has been a long time attendant of River Pretty, and doesn't think he could have accomplished either degree without the constant feedback, encouragement, and love found at the retreat. He sincerely wishes he had mutant powers, especially the ability to teleport, or super speed, because that would save a lot of time and he procrastinates to a level that may be considered irresponsible.

Andrew Marshall has lived in Oklahoma for the last nine years, but grew up on the beaches of Southern California. His collection of short stories, Simple Pleasures, was published in 2015 by ELJ press. His work is published or forthcoming in *The Fiddlehead, Appalachian Heritage, Red Wheelbarrow, Queen Mob's Teahouse, theNewerYork, Fiction Attic, Austin Review,* and *The Vestal Review.*

John R. Monagle: I am a native of Las Cruces, New Mexico. I reside in Rockville, Maryland and work at The Library Of Congress. I am a two-time Jenny McKean Moore Fellow at The George Washington University. I am pursuing a Master of Fine Arts Degree at Vermont College of Fine Arts. I have published poems in *Wordwrights* in 2002, and *Bourgeron* in 2010, *The Edge Literary Review* as well as a poem to be published in a forthcoming issue of *Two Hawks Quarterly*.

Annie Newcomer lives in Prairie Village, Kansas with her husband, David. They have been married for thirty- six years. Her participation in the generative poetry workshops at *River Pretty* motivated her response piece in this anthology, *Paddle Shots 2*. Interacting with the other writers, learning from the talented professors, hearing the words of the community of writers, while living in the poetic scene which is *River Pretty*, expanded her ability to appreciate this craft and better understand the magic of poetry. She is grateful for this experience.

Bill Oakley is an old wood's hippie living in cultural isolation in the Ozark hills. Through the input of his mentor, Lee Busby, he has been able to expand his ability to express his inner soul through lyric poetry.

Todd Osborne was born in Nashville, TN and is currently pursuing a PhD at the Center for Writers at the University of

Southern Mississippi. His poems have previously appeared in *Juked, Cargo Literary, Slipstream Quarterly*, and elsewhere.

J.T. Robertson is the author of the novella *The Memory Thieves* (2014) published by Black Hill Press. His work has also appeared in *Jelly Bucket, The Louisville Review, The MacGuffin, Moon City Review, McSweeney's Internet Tendency*, and other publications. J.T. holds a B.A. in creative writing from Missouri State University and funds his fiction-writing habit by working at a nonprofit in St. Louis. He is a regular attendee of the River Pretty Writers Retreat, and currently lives in Sycamore Hills, Missouri with his supportive wife Pamela and three entirely unpredictable cats. He is currently writing his first full-length novel.

Allen Ross: After over 700 songs, 16 music CD's, 4 screen plays, two Children's Books, 330 cartoon frames (enough for a daily calendar) of Mariachi Hell, 78 3-dimensional framed trash-art paintings for a Tarot deck of cards, a Book of Sonnets Sonnet, Allen is attempting to compose a poem from every poetic form each year until he becomes Poet Laureate of Greene County.

Sophfronia Scott is author of the novel *All I Need to Get By*. Her work has appeared in *Killens Review of Arts & Letters, Saranac Review, Numéro Cinq, Ruminate, Barnstorm Literary Journal, Sleet Magazine, NewYorkTimes.com*, and *O, The Oprah Magazine*. She lives in Sandy Hook, Connecticut and is on the faculty of Regis University's Mile-High MFA in Denver, Colorado.

Heather Sharfeddin is the author of four novels about the Pacific Northwest. Her work has earned starred reviews from *Kirkus Reviews* and *Library Journal*, has been honored with an Erick Hoffer award and at the New York and San Francisco Book Festivals, as well as the Pacific Northwest Book Sellers Association. She holds an MFA in writing from Vermont College of Fine Arts and a PhD in Creative Writing from Bath Spa University (Bath, England). She has taught creative writing at Randolph Macon College, University of Arkansas at Little Rock, and is currently an adjunct professor at Linfield College. For more information about her writing visit www.sharfeddin.com.

Sue William Silverman is the author of three memoirs: *The Pat Boone Fan Club: My Life as a White Anglo-Saxon Jew* was a finalist in *Foreword Review's* IndieFab Book of the Year Award; *Because I Remember Terror, Father, I Remember You* won the AWP Award in Creative Nonfiction; and *Love Sick: One Woman's Journey through Sexual Addiction* is also a Lifetime TV movie. Her other books include *Fearless Confessions: A Writer's Guide to Memoir,* and the poetry collection *Hieroglyphics in Neon.* Sue teaches in the MFA in Writing program at Vermont College of Fine Arts. www.SueWilliamSilverman.com

Sierra Sitzes is Graduate Student at Missouri State University where she teaches both Composition and Creative Writing. She attended River Pretty 2 and 6, and was the fiction scholarship recipient at River Pretty 8.

Andy Smart, the bearded poet.

Debbie Theiss is an emerging poet. She won 3rd place in the Japanese Haiku Festival Contest and has published poems in the Skinny Journal and the I-70 Review (September, 1016). She enjoys nature, hiking, bicycling, and gardening.

Michaella A Thornton stumbled upon the amazing River Pretty writing community when she fell in love with an essay Jennifer Murvin published in *The Sun.* Kella is super grateful to spend time in the Ozarks with her best friend Mary, talented writers, and generous faculty who have inspired big breakthroughs in her work (thank you, Jen and Rich). In October 2015, Kella won a prose scholarship at RP9 and, in August 2016, she has been invited to study with Dinty W. Moore and Mark Doty at "Iota: the conference of short prose" on Campobello Island, New Brunswick, Canada. Somehow Robert Olen Butler likes her stuff, and her flash fiction has been a two-time finalist for *The Southeast Review's* World's Best Short-Short Story Contest in 2014 and 2015. This year, 2016, she plans on winning the damn contest. Her website is michaellathornton.com

Robert Vivian is the author of *The Tall Grass Trilogy—The Mover of Bones, Lamb Bright Saviors,* and *Another Burning Kingdom,* in addition to the novel *Water and Abandon.* He's also written two books of meditative essays, *Cold Snap as Yearning* and *The Least Cricket of Evening.* His most recent collection of prose poems, *Mystery My Country,* will be published in 2016, along with *Traversings,* a new book co-written with Richard Jackson.

Jan A. Way is a retired District Judge from Kansas.

Lee, Chaz, Steve, Rich, Jen, and Ian are the core faculty of River Pretty and are proud as all hell of the community that has been built around this small dream that we all shared (and still do!), and we hope to be able to do this until the cows come home (which should be a while, since none of us own cows).